Return To Emerald Isle

4/12/17

Chase,
Hope you enjoy!

Thomas P.

Return To Emerald Isle

Thomas P. Gill

ISBN: 1542753775
ISBN 13: 9781542753777
Library of Congress Control Number: 2017901947
CreateSpace Independent Publishing Platform
North Charleston, South Carolina

Writing about Emerald Isle, The Crystal Coast, and Eastern North Carolina, while incorporating stories from family and friends, is a passion made possible through the support of many people. Key to ensuring Return to Emerald Isle is enjoyable is my editor, N. K. Wagner, editor of Page and Spine, who provided direct and constructive content and style feedback to my numerous drafts. Beta readers, including my wife, daughters, brother, sister, and mother, Billie-Fae Gill, an excellent author in her own right, were invaluable in providing input and helping move to publication. A special thanks to author, Dr. Curt Finch, and his wife, Debbie, owners of Emerald Isle Books and Toys, for their tremendous support of my writing endeavor. I sincerely appreciate the many readers of my first novel, The Bridge, for their comments and suggestions, which I have considered for inclusion in Return To Emerald Isle.

"I haven't been in a storm like this in years. ABS, I'm really scared. And now, living right on the beach... Should we have evacuated?"

"Baby, nothing to do now but sit tight," ABS replies calmly. "Kirby, you and I grew up at the coast and have gone through plenty of these. Wilmington had their share of hurricanes, just like I saw in New Bern." He hugs me close and whispers, "This time tomorrow it'll be over. You'll think it was just a dream. Promise! Let's go upstairs and join the party."

Grams and Journey, her only grandson, sip lemonade while Mom and Dad opt for more mature beverages. Everyone is glued to the television. A collective gasp escapes as the Storm Tracker Special Announcement interrupts the regularly scheduled news.

We interrupt our ongoing weather report to bring this emergency update. New models indicate Hurricane Michele has outer bands of sustained wind over one hundred and fifty-six miles per hour and is expected to make landfall on Bogue Banks. All people in the Channel 7 viewing area must seek shelter immediately. Landfall is anticipated between Atlantic Beach and the eastern edge of Bogue Banks, near Fort Macon, at seven o'clock tonight. Due to the expected high tide at eight o'clock, the storm surge may exceed fifteen feet. Prepare for flooding. Tornados and water spouts are possible, as is a power outage on the island. Do not venture outside for any reason. Injury or death from flying debris, drowning, or electrical shock are real possibilities. Local authorities warn: no emergency responders will come out until the storm passes. We repeat…

Journey's face is drained of color. My baby boy is shark-belly white. Grams huddles closer to Mom while Dad continues his limping pace, back and forth across the dining area.

"Okay everyone, we just need to stay calm. Journey, honey it'll be alright. We have a sturdy house and plenty of supplies."

"But Mom, what about the sea turtles?" Journey cries. "Their nests are my responsibility. I bet no one covered them."

The lights flicker and fail. The increasing winds buffet the house while windows, doors, and ceilings creak and groan. Grams shrieks and Mom begins to cry silently, "We should have left. It's just like Hugo in '89."

"It's okay guys," Dad says peering out the window. "A transformer blew across the street. Our generator will be on in ten seconds…"

Table of Contents

Chapter 1

Pilots and Aviators

Very few humans, other than death row inmates, know exactly how long they have remaining on earth. Is it fifty years, or perhaps they've already taken their last breath? Sam and I committed on our wedding night to treat each second as our last. I just didn't think it would come this soon.

Seventeen years ago, I married my high school and college sweetheart, Marine pilot Sam Fontaine, the only man I ever knew or loved! Sam grew up in Emerald Isle, North Carolina where during summer breaks I vacationed at my grandparent's beach home. I loved growing up at Topsail Beach, just an hour south, and cherished even more that we found each other on this magical island during the summer of my sixteenth year. Ensuing summers allowed us to explore and get to appreciate each other in so many ways. Before we knew it, high school and college flew by and we were standing at the altar, vowing to share our love and lives together.

After college, we traveled the world as Sam pursued his military career. I put my nursing career on hold when we were blessed with our beautiful son, Journey. Many military spouses do this when they are just starting out and we were only two years into Sam's service. We named Journey to honor Sam's best friend and partly to avoid offending either grandfather.

Deacon "Journey" Studley barely graduated from the US Naval Academy and met Sam a year later in pilot training at Pensacola Naval Air Station. A scholar athlete football player when Navy was a conference powerhouse, Deac was much more the latter, finishing academically near the bottom of his class. Despite this, the selection rate to attend this prestigious school ensured many companies and airlines would offer him a job after his military obligation.

A brash, some say cocky, naval aviator (they can't call themselves pilots like the Air Force or Marines for some reason), Deac won his aviator call sign "Journey" during his pilot training graduation solo. He'd hoped to use his nick name "Stud" like he had in high school. Deac's actions during his solo flight changed that! While flying cross country to earn the coveted naval aviator flight wings, Deac took liberties and buzzed several of his favorite places including his high school and his girlfriend's house just outside Gadsden, Alabama. Gadsden was filed on his flight plan, but Deac's high school was certainly not; especially when he dipped his wings just thirty feet above the football field. Anxious observers reported he was almost close enough to score a field goal when he flew over the posts.

Saluting the practicing cheerleading squad really got people's attention. Multiple frantic phone calls from local authorities alerted the flight training base resulting in Deac's near early discharge. Thankfully, a high-ranking officer in the training command accepted Deac's apology and promise to "color inside the lines" going forward. For his transgression, Deac earned the flight call sign "Journey" to remind him of his traveling *mistake* throughout his Navy career. Ironically, this call sign became a term of endearment as many junior pilots enjoyed getting their picture taken with Deac as he advanced in military rank. That was certainly not the last time he deviated from regulations.

As a career Marine pilot family, Sam, Journey and I were fortunate to travel around the world as Sam sought out the most difficult and trying assignments. From a combat crew flying position at Cherry Point Marine Corps Air Station in Havelock, North Carolina to a squadron command position in Yuma, Arizona, we loved our exciting military life. Sam's relocation to San Diego was what the military refers to as a "career broadening" opportunity. *No problems there for sure – broaden away!* Later, Sam passed on an opportunity to serve as Executive Officer for the Blue Angels Navy flight demonstration squadron deciding instead to stay in combat leadership roles. Timing is everything in both military and civilian careers and this decision was critical. Because they were senior aviators and current in their aircraft requirements, Deac and Sam were instrumental in helping defeat ISIS in the short-lived air battle that should have been waged years earlier. As a combat experienced ace with seven confirmed kills, Sam eventually became a "top gun" test pilot – best in the Marine Corps – and handpicked to be the first Marine to lead a joint service test squadron at Edwards Air Force base in California. Sam was a born leader!

The moment I saw Sam, as a fifteen-year-old rising sophomore with raging hormones during my summer visit to Pappy and Grams, I knew I loved him. His "wingman" since I crashed Pappy's car over the Emerald Isle Langston Bridge in one of my life's defining moments, we cherished and cared for each other steadfastly. Sam helped nurse me back to emotional and physical health following that painful episode. My pilot is gone now and I was unable to help him. By returning to the island, perhaps I can help Mom, Dad and Grams.

Dad's mobility has improved tremendously. His spinal fusion surgery and experimental exoskeleton, outfitted him by the East Carolina University Medical School orthopedic surgeons and rehabilitation experts, has been almost miraculous. He can do so much more than anyone thought possible after breaking his neck when he jumped off the Emerald Isle bridge to save me. Dad continues to surprise everyone as he relearns how to drive, swim, fish, and even use a paddleboard. His slight limp is the only discernible evidence of the incident. Always modest, Dad likes to say his situation is simply a "First World Problem."

"People all over the world would love to have my challenges," he quietly comments when people ask him how he's doing. His biggest regret is not being able to surf. Likewise, he can't drive his restored 1952 jeep on the beach during the winter months. The deep ruts made in the sand by four-wheel drive vehicles make for hard jolts that are too dangerous. A spill could reinjure his neck. And now – now -- that I'm coming home, I'll be able to help around the house until Journey and I can get settled. Pappy's Place, named for my grandfather, is huge and a handful to manage.

I can clean and help in the kitchen a little. Little is good enough, as my biggest failure to Sam was never learning to cook. I can definitely check out the pool and ensure it's in good shape. That won't be too difficult a task as I enjoy checking out pools. The reason for our return to the Crystal Coast is beyond sad, but I do look forward to being able to help my aging family. And I'll get to spend time with Grams, my favorite person other than Journey. My maternal grandmother has always been my confidant. She ensured I was ready for my first date with Sam nearly a lifetime ago. I love her direct, forceful yet fun-loving and adventuresome manners, and look forward to sharing her with Journey.

At five foot nine and one hundred thirty-five pounds, Journey is the spittin' image of Sam. He has the same golfer physique Sam was always trying to enhance. Both of them were unable to bulk up even after buying tons of weights and trying the newest weight-gaining shake. What a great problem to have. I sort of like my guys being able to have a conversation and buy clothes off the rack rather than flexing and strutting all the time. Like Sam, Journey has the same wavy blonde hair that flips up on the back of his neck and hangs just over his eyebrows. Once the Emerald Isle sun gives him a rich "coat of tan" as my great grandma would say, I'm sure he will have to fight off the girls.

Today, Journey and I, without Sam, embark on our return trek to our Crystal Coast. Unsure of the unknown -- we've always had the Marine Corps and Sam to guide us - we don't know what we'll do once we get there. For sure, Grams, Mom and Dad, and the rest of the family will be, as the song says, "Wind Beneath Our Wings." Perhaps we can support them too.

If it wasn't for heading back to Emerald Isle with Journey, I'd go to sleep and never wake up. *God, I miss Sam so much.*

Chapter 2

Karma

Why does stuff happen to me? I always color between the lines and nearly got straight "A"s. I went to school every day for twelve years – never sick and didn't skip classes. Never got suspended. No drugs and only a sip of beer, shared with Pappy and Dad. On the honor roll every term, I was class salutatorian and earned several college scholarships. I say my prayers religiously every night and keep the commandments - at least most of them. I floss at least daily and wash my hands whenever I use the restroom. I don't jay walk, rarely speed, don't run "yellows", and always stop for pedestrians! I practice the Golden Rule - not the 20th century version that says, "Do Unto Others *before* They Do Unto You"! I read "Red Sea Rules" as my daily devotional guide and as a teenager even wore a True Love Waits ring – the modern-day chastity belt. Most of my teenage friends were a bit liberal defining chastity, perhaps because political leaders seem to have this challenge, too. Not me! On my wedding night I was as pure as the driven snow - and so was Sam!

So, why, then? Why does this dark cloud hang over my head? Where does Karma come off being my traveling companion? I never did anything to her. Is she waiting for my screw up to justify all she has already done? We've been acquaintances since I was fifteen. I thought, perhaps, when Sam and I got married, I had vanquished her. For years she must have found another roost. Recently, it seems she's found her way back.

Karma first appeared when she led Sam and I to the video where I learned my "dad" really wasn't my dad. My birth father was shot by a neighbor shortly after I was conceived. How did Karma show up? I wrecked Pappy's beautiful car off the high rise Emerald Isle Bridge. If that wasn't enough this tragedy resulted in my "dad" being paralyzed when he jumped in to save me. Now, my husband, my first and only true love, has been stolen from me in a test flight accident. You can bet if I ever see Karma again I will give her a piece of my mind.

Pappy, my maternal grandfather, used to say, "The only thing you *HAVE* to do is pay taxes and die." I never gave much thought to the dying part. Who does, when they're young and invincible? Sam and I were deeply in love, proud parents of a great kid, active with friends on military bases and in the local communities, and enjoying exciting world travels -- courtesy of dear old Uncle Sam. My Sam's military career was nearly perfect. Below the zone promotions, head test pilot for the Marine Corps, and on track for career broadening assignments at The

Pentagon. All of this changed just a few short months ago when Karma reared her ugly head again. Sam didn't come back from what was to be his last test flight. I guess it really was…his last flight.

Posthumously promoted, Sam would have been one of the youngest Colonels in the Marine Corps. With transfer orders to Washington, DC, I had planned to reignite my nursing career at the Walter Reed National Military Medical Center. I was excited to be reporting to the med/surg department and restarting the career that had been on hold as we relocated from base to base across the world to advance Sam's military career. Ditching his experimental jet to protect the millions of people living in LA was absolutely expected of Sam -- but how I wish he was here now.

Chapter 3

Emerald Isle Bound

Yep, Pappy, "taxes and dying." Sam and I always paid our taxes and were certainly fine with paying the other debt too. Just not this early. So, now Journey and I begin our lives without him. I glance for the last time at the stagnant uniformity of military housing before beginning the drive from Edwards Air Force Base to LAX. Everything appears picture perfect. Lawns are manicured and mailboxes stand at attention as we slowly drive down winding roads. My eyes sting as this chapter folds into the next – Journey's and my new life, alone. I turn the radio on extra loud to drown out the silence. Oh My God! Chills run down my spine as Clapton's biggest hit, "Tears in Heaven" begins to play. Like the singer asks, I wonder if Sam would know me in heaven?

Soul wrenching lyrics pound into my brain as we depart this life and begin a new one. As the base's front gate and the creature comforts of being a Marine pilot's family for the past seventeen years grow smaller in the rearview mirror, I allow myself to shed a tear, hoping Journey will not notice.

He does.

Scooching next to me on the bench seat, Journey tightens his seat belt and places his hand gently on my shoulder. How can this teenager, full of anger with the loss of his buddy, know exactly the right thing to do, at the right time? Reaching over, I brush back a tear from his cheek as we silently share this time together. Cars pass on either side as I careen through the Mohave Desert at a decidedly unsafe forty miles per hour. I can't even understand why everyone is honking. Lost on me at the moment as we depart on California state highway 58 is that we are returning to Emerald Isle on North Carolina state highway 58. Karma? Omen? Is there a message here?

At nearly fifteen, Journey is old enough to be a man, but still young enough to need his mom occasionally. This is one of those times. Ironically, I was fifteen when I met Sam one wonderful summer while visiting Emerald Isle. Seems like last week - but oceans of water have passed under the bridge since then.

My mind wanders further. Losing Sam a few months ago ripped my heart out. I'll never find another man like him! His selflessness cost me the most, but I am so proud of him. I recall his eulogy as the crowd of military mourners openly wept, listening to the command center's recording of his heroics. I'll never forget it after hearing it replayed in my head so many times and can only guess what was going on in Sam's mind.

"Mayday, Mayday. Command Post. Par Man 59 declares in-flight emergency. Catastrophic power loss. Flight controls inop –unable to RTB. Flying a rock! Repeat: no steering; unable to return to base. Dumping fuel.... Ditching in 180… Copy?"

"Roger Par Man 59. Command Post copies: No Power; no control; ditching in Los Angeles Bay. Rescue helo and Coast Guard cutter enroute. ETA seven minutes."

"Sam, hang in there buddy. We're coming for you."

"Roger Deac. Engine flared at Mach 3. Hydraulic leak. Auxiliary power out. Canopy inop. Ditching fast and hard. Watch over Kirby and Journey.... I'm counting on you."

"Not happening. Not today Bud. Pull up and glide that rock in – like Sully on the Hudson. See you soon."

"Par Man 59, report status," the Command Post operator directed. By now, all hands focused on the radar blip free falling over LA. The silence is deafening.

"Command One, clear LA Bay. Not going to make it; ditching in five. My love to Kirby and Journey. God bless you all…."

Radio silence…

Commander Deacon Studley, Sam Fontaine's best friend and our only child's namesake, looks at the Command Post operator as the staffers hover around the console. He shakes his head.

One short week later, while holding Mom's hand and resting my other one on fourteen-year-old Journey's trembling shoulders, we join hundreds of military personnel from US and foreign services in the Edward Air Force Base cavernous aircraft hangar. Home of the US Air Force Test Pilot School, Sam had been the first Marine pilot to lead a joint service test fighter squadron at this elite California training base. Typical of Sam's career, he was "first" in many challenges and being groomed for senior command. The California desert sun made the open hangar almost unbearable while the uniformed servicemen and women stoically stand at attention in silent salute to a hero. Vice President of the United States Vic O. Kelley tears up while posthumously awarding Sam the Navy Distinguished Service Medal.

Looking sharp in her perfectly tailored uniform, the female naval officer's voice breaks slightly as she reads the medal's citation:

"In recognition of United States Marine Corps Lieutenant Colonel Samuel M. Fontaine's exceptional valor and superior service...." I must have blacked out briefly as I heard her concluding with, "...on behalf of a grateful nation and the citizens of Los Angeles...."*

Vice President Kelley continues his prepared remarks praising Sam for ditching in the ocean, saving countless lives while sacrificing his own.

Half-heartedly, I listen to the other speakers. Senators, mayors, and military dignitaries drone on seemingly to capitalize on our misfortune. Our good friend, Sam's mentor and the base commander, Major General Dan Cooper, barely retains his composure while sharing how Sam was the son he never had. My mind drifts. It is hard to believe seventeen years have flown by so quickly - only to end like this. Three years from retirement, we planned for our military pension to finance our return to Emerald Isle, together.

What's it been? Twenty-four years since we innocently stumbled on our first ceremonial funeral video – the one of my birth father, a Marine and fireman - shot to death by a vigilante neighbor. Who would dream I might tragically lose another man so important to me? God knows I loved Sam. How many times had I begged him to stop flying? Being a Marine and pilot was tough enough. Being a test pilot increased the odds of disaster!

Other than learning of the deceit surrounding my birth father's death, listening to the radio transmission the day of Sam's accident was the most difficult day of my life. Trying hard to move past this tragedy, Journey and I are moving back to the Crystal Coast – not the homecoming we had planned – but still a homecoming to family and comfortable surroundings.

I knew something terrible would eventually happen. Sam loved to fly almost as much as he loved Emerald Isle and the Crystal Coast. He told me many times if something "happened" he wanted to be laid to rest near the

Bogue Banks pier in the Atlantic Ocean. For eternity, he wants to sense the changing tides, hear the roar of the waves, and feel the warm sun. Sam feared burial with others he did not know in perfect lines of white granite markers in the cold of a national cemetery. Thankfully, the Marine Corps did not push this issue. Although Sam was a war hero and a rising senior officer, Deac convinced the military leadership a private burial was most important to my family.

The noise of several hundred chairs jostling startles me to the present as I realize everyone is rising to stand at attention – to pay their respect one last time. The end is near, in more ways than one.

Squeezing Journey's shoulder a little harder and feeling several hands on my waist and back, I steel myself for the final tribute. In the distance, a lone bugler surreally begins to play TAPS... I loved Sam deeply, but I want this to finish quickly.

Thankfully, Journey and I have each other to look after. And, of course Deacon and his wife Sally, who have been such great long-time friends and recent angels, promise to "be there for us." Family and friends will be looking after us too when we get home.

Home... Emerald Isle. Sam loved the island of his birth, and, although it is expensive to live there, we look forward to coming home. People don't get rich on a military salary but with careful planning we'll be able to afford to live on the island. Sam's Servicemen's Group Life insurance and Dad's portfolio advice through the years will keep us comfortable. My in-laws offered for me to take over their family restaurant, *Chowdaheads*. It's been in their family for more than three decades and they are getting up in years. I thought about it, but that was to be Sam's legacy. I don't think I can stomach the daily reminders. Eventually, I may take a job. I'll have to stay busy, or I may go insane.

Aunt Reagan, Mom's younger sister, continues to manage the Emerald Isle Book Store Grams bought fifteen years ago. While expanding and updating the store, they continue to maintain the forty-year-old family friendly atmosphere. Perhaps she will need my help on a part time basis. We'll see. For now, we just need to get home. And, of course, there is always nursing. I love caring for patients. I enjoyed taking care of the infants in the neo-natal intensive care unit before Sam's career really started taking off. But that was a lifetime ago – much has changed and I'm not sure I have the physical or emotional stamina to take care of anybody else.

Like in an hour glass, the sands of time slip through imperceptibly. Nearly six months have passed since Sam died. Military families normally have to move out of their house within thirty days of a service member's death. The Air Force leaders were so generous allowing us to remain on base as we completed plans to move home. Home to Emerald Isle. It seems like years since we've been there.

And, like playing Monopoly with my cousins, this nearly two-hour drive through the sterile California countryside from Edwards Air Force Base to LAX is boring. I hate these kinds of drives while others relax and enjoy the countryside. Not me, the "energizer bunny." I need to see other people, cars, billboards; even some trash on the side of the road would be appreciated. The long winding curves through the California hills almost make me nauseous.

I bet the nearly five-hour flight will be even more boring. Thankfully, first class seats, compliments of Deac and Sally, will help make our return a little bit easier. Journey is excited to be headed back to Emerald Isle, too. Of course he misses his dad greatly, but kids are so resilient. Then again, I'm not sure the shock has really sunk in. We'll see. As we enter the Los Angeles metropolitan area, I remember how congested and scary these roads can be. There are more highways here than in almost any other city in the world, sometimes with six or more lanes moving in each direction. I've driven in Boston, Chicago, New York and other big cities. They are crazy, too. I'm in LA now, so these are the worst! Here, the highways don't seem to follow any pattern, twisting and turning with freeway on and off ramps every few miles. It appears the builders just poured concrete on the hills and let it roll until it stopped. Then they built the city around the roads, placing multiple signs to confuse drivers more. Adding to the scariness -- is that even a word? -- are the idiot wannabe NASCAR drivers whizzing by at break-neck speeds while I'm simply trying to make it to the airport within the posted speed limit.

Finally, I see a directional sign indicating the LAX exit is in three miles. Even better, I spy a Hertz rental van which will eventually get me to the airport if I follow it. It is just a few vehicles in front. I remember driving here to drop Sam off a few times. It's confusing. LAX seems like the Atlanta interstate intersection referred to as Spaghetti Junction. Road signs point this way and that. Visitors can spend hours lost in the maze. I've heard of more than one traveler who missed a flight by not getting off the merry-go-round in time. Sam shared his trick about following the rental agency vans - they always go to the airport and back to the rental lot. So, "follow one and you will get to one or the other," he told me. While my phone GPS came in handy navigating to this point, I now put my trust in my angel, Sam. I need to return my rental anyway. I follow the van.

Good move! After turning in our rental, we hop on board the Hertz shuttle. In just a few minutes we arrive at the American Airlines terminal. So far, so good. Now to get through the always-invasive "TSA Gestapo" and board our flight. Talk about good fortune. Perhaps someone called ahead. Our First Class tickets rated personal escort through a special pre-check line. In less than twenty minutes we're waiting to board. Never before has this happened for me. Then again, never before has my husband died for his country.

LAX is a melting pot of people, much like New York City was during the mass immigration of the 1800s. If I have to be here, at least I can look for celebrities. What an exciting and fun place to people watch – sort of like old fashioned window shopping when people drove or walked around store fronts looking at what they might buy, if only they could afford it. People come in all forms at LAX. Every color and size; happy to sad; scared and excited; tired and refreshed; sometimes, even dirty or clean. One remembers when you get stuck beside the former. There are plenty of in-shape people flying out of LAX as well as out of shape; small and tall; families with lots of luggage with screaming babies and businessmen scurrying to their next flight carrying a single briefcase. There are eccentric looking and normal looking (whatever that is anymore) people; women AND men with tattoos and earrings everywhere, including places normal people don't usually have them like old fashioned carnival performers, airport and airline employees, and of course, hidden among all of them are the VIPs. LA is home to so many celebrities who want to be seen, but complain they want to remain invisible. They try to hide in plain sight disguising themselves by wearing normal fashions, but they are there. Sometimes they sneak onto flights from the clubs with an airline escort while other times they simply board like normal folks and try to fit in.

Pappy told me stories about seeing unique characters while waiting on flights at LAX. Two of them included former heavy weight "rassling" champions Rick Flair from Charlotte and Jesse Ventura, who is also the former governor of Minnesota. He flew beside both of them during separate flights to North Carolina. He shared some interesting stories that I can't repeat here. One of his other celebrity sightings included a group of gorgeous Swedish cheerleaders. They were extremely excited as they were on their way home from Las Vegas having won the international competition. I don't recall Grams being a great fan of that story!

Scanning the crowds, I hope to spy a VIP or at least divert my mind from thinking about Sam. Interrupting my focus, a well-groomed and articulate flight attendant leaned in toward me asking, "Excuse me ma'am, are you Mrs. Kirby Fontaine?"

Looking up from my seat and thinking it may be time to board I answer, "Yes sir and this is my son, Journey."

"Hello Mrs. Fontaine. Journey. We're pleased to have you fly with us tonight. The Captain would like to offer you an opportunity to pre-board. We are so proud to have you on our flight and so sorry for your loss."

Taken by surprise, I stutter while acknowledging his offer and condolences. "Th… th… thanks so much. This is so kind. Yes, we would love to board early."

"Great. Please follow me. May I help you with your bags?"

Chapter 4

LAX to Charlotte

American Airlines Captain Kevin Crutchfield flew with Sam during the Third Gulf War. Once our new President demonstrated the necessary resolve to ensure peace throughout the world it took only thirty-five days to eradicate the terroristic regime. Our superior air power and occupying ground forces quickly broke the enemy with very few American casualties. Like Sam and Deac, Crutch and other war heroes won't mention their involvement – sometimes, not even if you ask.

Once, when Deac was visiting a few years ago, I accidentally overheard Sam talking about the war with him and Journey. They were in the garage while I folded clothes in the adjoining laundry room. I'm sure Sam didn't know I was nearby. He never talked with me about his time in the war. I felt bad that Sam wouldn't share with me, but I was elated to secretly witness this male bonding with Journey. I hadn't thought about that until now.

I remember, then twelve-year old Journey, asking something like, "Dad, how'd you do it?" Sam and Deac, to their credit kept the answer PG-rated without the gruesome detail I'm sure they might have shared with other veterans.

"Son," Deac started, "your dad kicked their butts. He was the squadron lead plane during multiple sorties delivering huge payloads of smart bombs. Before we were born, the Air Force had a campaign in Vietnam they called "Rolling Thunder". Ours was sort of like that. We threw everything at them and blew them off the map!" Deac was toned down, but still a little dramatic.

Sam calmed Deac a bit adding, "J, we broke their commitment by breaking their backs! Most importantly, my entire squadron came home alive."

Always needing to have the last word Deac added, "Journey, you might not realize this yet but your dad is a national treasure. An honest to God hero! Many pilots and support crew members credit their lives and war time success to his leadership. He won't talk about it but never forget what I told you."

I never mentioned my inadvertent eavesdropping to Sam or Journey but knew through other medal citations and his career advancements how much his team and military leaders thought of Sam.

Of course! This helps explain our personal escort and expedited process through the TSA line.

As we take our seats, a handsome flight officer about my age, wearing the traditional black and white airline captain's uniform, approached. Holding his hat while offering his other hand he said, "Good evening Mrs. Fontaine, Journey. Welcome aboard. I'm Captain Crutchfield. My friends call me Crutch."

"Kirby" I correct softly. "Please call me Kirby. It's nice to meet you, Crutch."

Smiling, he glanced at me, then back to Journey and continued. "Journey, I flew with your dad before I got out of the Marine Corps. He was a great man, pilot, and leader. I'm proud to have served with him and so sorry for your loss. I'll be taking you all the way to Charlotte this evening. Is there anything we can do to make you comfortable?"

"Thanks Crutch. We really appreciate your kindness. Journey and I are fine but I'll let you know if we need anything." Journey smiled appreciatively but remained silent. *He gets this way whenever his dad's death is mentioned.*

"Anything for Par Man 59." Using Sam's call sign convinced me Crutch had flown with Sam.

I can tell Deac is still pulling strings to make sure we are taken care of. Angels on my shoulders, I think.

"Oh, Crutch, there is one thing. Do you think Journey could get a cockpit tour? You know Sam only flew fighters."

"Absolutely! Journey, want to check out our Dreamliner 787? We'll need to be quick before the rest of the passengers begin boarding. Since 9-11, the airlines have been very strict about visits in the cockpit, once boarding begins."

Journey's affirmative answer came almost before he finished the question. Captain Crutchfield happily obliged and off they went.

Journey toured the cockpit and our flying companions began boarding. I took notice of the cabin while settling in. Pillows and blankets had been removed from most airlines over the past decade, especially for those traveling on military orders or in coach class. The front of this plane, reserved for first class passengers, is quite a bit different. Creature comforts are not in short supply. The Mimosa offered as the attendants moved throughout the cabin was delightful. I slip off my shoes and recline my extra wide leather seat to the full extent – nearly completely parallel with the floor. *This might not be such a bad ride after all.* As passengers file past, I busy myself with the seat, magazines, and anything else I can find, conscious that most passengers look enviously at those of us sitting in the front of the plane.

Journey returns in a few minutes and asks, "Hey Mom, are you going to sleep?" You know you have to sit up for take-off."

Mashing the button to return my seat to the normal upright position I reply, "I know sweetheart. I'm just getting acquainted with the seat controls. We usually flew in coach when... Well, you know, when Dad was here."

I loved Sam but when will it stop? Really; even getting comfortable in a plane? Hoping Journey does not see my tears or hear the tremor in my voice, I ask, "How was the tour? Did you get to sit in the Captain's Chair?"

"It was great, Mom. The cockpit is huge. Lots bigger than the fighters Dad let me sit in. But I liked Dad's better!"

Maybe he had not seen my tears. *Journey is so brave and thoughtful.*

"Captain Crutch. He said to call him that, okay? He knows so much about flying these big planes. He said we might be able to fly in a simulator if we ever visit Charlotte. He lives close to the Charlotte Motor Speedway and said we might be able to go see a race, too."

"That's wonderful Journey. Sure, if Crutch wants you to call him that I'm fine with it."

I haven't seen him this excited for weeks. It's so nice to see Journey animated about anything right now although I would prefer it not be about flying! Talking about the future. That's a switch. He's been so melancholy.

"We'll see about getting back to Charlotte sometime - that sounds like fun and there really is a lot to do there. For now, let's get ready to take off. Grab your book and anything else you might need for the next few minutes. Don't forget to turn off your cell too. Wake me up when we get there. I'm going to try to take a nap."

"Okay Mom. Just one more thing. Captain Crutchfield said there is a possible hurricane developing in the Caribbean. It won't impact our flight but we might see some of it a few days. That's pretty exciting."

"Believe me Journey, that's the last thing I want to see. I've seen enough cyclones, hurricanes, typhoons…

remember, we even went through a tsunami when we lived in the Azores? That was when you were very little, and it was really scary."

"Try to get some sleep, Journey. It's a long trip," I added smiling inwardly as I turned my head into the chair's cushioned headrest. Coincidentally, playing softly over the intercom as we taxi toward the runway is James Taylor's hit, "Carolina In My Mind." No doubt this is a North Carolina flight crew. Many other things begin to race through my mind as the back of my eyes begin their date with my eyelids.

Chapter 5

Charlotte: Home Sweet Home

Oh My God! *How can someone sleep so deep? I missed dinner, the movie, and free snacks.* Waking up after the nearly five-hour long, but thankfully uneventful flight, I coax my legs to listen to my brain so I can walk the twenty steps to the first class cabin restroom. *A quick straightening of my hair and reapplication of makeup and I might pass for a pretty woman. Ugh! Well, I don't know anyone in Charlotte anyway.*

As we quickly deplane, Captain Crutchfield greets us at the exit ramp. "Hope I see you both again," he said holding my hand a little longer than comfortable. *His eyes seem to be saying a bit more than his words. Maybe I'm just really exhausted. It has been a long day.*

"Thanks Crutch," Journey and I say at nearly the same time. The queue grows behind us and I'm ready to get to the next plane. "The flight was great although I slept through much of it. Thanks again for showing Journey the cockpit. Get some rest. You have to be tired."

The ancient agent reviewing boarding passes as we enter the terminal said we had enough time to catch our connecting flight but, "Don't dally." *Who uses this term these days?* "Just get on the moving sidewalk until it ends," I hear as we briskly walk away.

"Easy enough," flipping him a thumbs up signal. I add, "Thank you," over my shoulder. He was bent over already looking at another passenger's boarding pass.

With our long legs, Journey and I are fast walkers. I glance at my phone and review my electronic boarding pass. It appears we have plenty of time. Not knowing where we are going makes me a bit unsure. "Let's go Bud."

I start toward the moving sidewalk, and in the back of my head hear Deac's reminder, "the sidewalks will take you all the way to the E terminal once you land in Charlotte." He thought of everything!

The Charlotte Douglas airport is enormous, even for experienced travelers. I learned, as I prepared for our trip, over forty-five million travelers fly through Charlotte every year. The D and E terminals are used for smaller commuter planes and personal "puddle jumpers" as Sam referred to them. These terminals are located at the furthest point from the main airport concourses and can take as much as fifteen minutes of race walking to reach them even when using the moving sidewalks. Specially equipped golf carts are also available for passengers with tight connections or having trouble walking. Thankfully, airport managers know the importance of communication. They have great signage posted for all the visitors, especially non-English speaking travelers.

It's tough enough to travel when one can speak the language. Watching the signs and riding the crawling sidewalk, I feel a little bit giddy. I guess everyone has experienced this feeling. It's like the end of the sixth or ninth grade. With summer signaling an exciting ninety days of fantastic adventures, I still remember the queasiness in my stomach as I thought about all the unknowns in my new school. Now I have a new world to confront.

Uncomfortable with these feelings, I'm still extremely elated to be coming home to Emerald Isle. Starting over, as trying as it may be, is not the primary issue. For now, I revel in the fact that we're almost home. Even the Charlotte airport offers familiar sights -- North Carolina style BBQ restaurants, marquees advertising the current Superbowl champion Carolina Panthers, and even a sign celebrating the 100th anniversary of Myrtle Beach, South Carolina. *Home, almost home.*

Journey said, "Look Mom! There's the Charlotte Motor Speedway Crutch mentioned. You loved it when you were a kid, according to Dad." He winched at the comment. *Yep, his absence hurts - especially when we have only recently begun to accept we are really on our own.*

Thomas P. Gill

"Yes, Journey, there's lots to do in North Carolina. But, first, we have to get home."

I'm beyond happy to see him excited; but don't want to make a big deal about it, yet. As we enter the three terminals' convergence, the crowd's hustle and bustle overshadow the melody emanating from a grand piano. Like a fine hotel ballroom, the lobby is several stories high. Appropriately hanging in the rafters is a full scale replica of the Wright Flyer flown by Orville and Wilbur Wright at Kitty Hawk over a hundred years ago. North Carolina claims them as their own, conveniently forgetting the bicycle shop brothers hailed from Ohio.

Reminiscent of my trip to New York City Grand Central Station, hundreds, if not thousands, of people appear to be purposefully headed in different directions. It looks like a bunch of busy bees. Sure, there are a few older passengers who seem to be taking longer looks at the monitors and a few young lovers strolling hand in hand seemingly unaware of the frenzy surrounding them. I used to be that person. Now I'm quickly moving to the former group. Moving slowly, come to think of it, I feel pretty tired. My snooze on the plane was just enough to make me crave more sleep.

I notice a row of white rocking chairs lining the moving sidewalk. Travelers rest and rock as they people-watch or look at departing planes. I have no idea why I remember something as trivial as this, but I do. These are *Troutman Chair* wooden rockers – well known as the "World's Best

Rockers." Still hand-crafted, using traditional furniture-making skills passed down through generations, these chairs are built just outside Pappy's hometown, Statesville, North Carolina. I remember Pappy proudly talking about how he and Grams worked at the plant when they were growing up. Both of their fathers were in the furniture business and *helped* them get summer jobs. Pappy would fondly reminisce how Troutman uses only North Carolina oak logs and prepares them from start to finish at their furniture plant. Cutting and curing their own lumber, Troutman Chair has made rocking chairs for nearly one hundred years. High society people, including President John F. Kennedy, and good ole boys, like Pappy, have long enjoyed the comfort of Troutman rockers. After purchasing P&P Chair Company, which made the original rocker for a young Senator Kennedy to ail his injured back, Troutman Chair Company continues the tradition of providing world class rockers throughout the world.

Thinking of Troutman reminds me of how close we are to Statesville and Pappy's people. Just forty minutes north on Interstate 77, Statesville, the "City of Progress", retains its small town charm. Over two hundred years old, its proximity to Charlotte and man-made Lake Norman, made in the late 1950s by damming up the Catawba River, offers much to do.

Just like Journey said but first we have to get home.

A little guilty, I realize I should have called and reminded Great Grandma, Pappy's mom, who is a young ninety-nine and still driving, that we are flying through Charlotte. With all of the security restrictions, we couldn't have visited easily, anyway. I would have hated going back through security again, before the next flight. Now that we are living only a five-hour drive away we can visit more often.

Like many military families, we missed lots of births, weddings, celebrations, and family reunions over the past seventeen years. Now Journey and I can spend time with his great uncles -- Pappy's brothers -- and all of the cousins. I remember getting to spend time with my cousins, especially at Emerald Isle! We really missed that over the last few years. Summer time on the island is best, but any time at Pappy's Place was simply magical: dances under the house, toasting s'mores in the fire pit, even skinny dipping with just the four of us cousins – thankfully we never got caught. Perhaps we'll not mention that last memory to Journey.

Pointing to the chairs, I said, "Hey Journey. Let's rest for a few minutes. We have time."

"Got it Mom. Snag a couple while I grab Auntie Annie's pretzels. We haven't had them in forever."

"Awesome. Be careful Honey," I yell over my shoulder walking hurriedly to secure the two vacant chairs near the end of the row. I almost gasp out loud as I sink into the hand-made wooden chair. Grams has Troutman rocking chairs at the beach house and I remember how wonderfully comfortable these rockers are as I close my eyes.

Chapter 6

Race

"Phew," I exclaim as we finally arrive at Gate 23 all the way at the end of Terminal E. Why do all the commuter planes fly out of the farthest gates? Stretching my legs by walking on the moving sidewalk was good for my circulation and my mind but after drinking large cokes with our pretzels and having to go -- we need to find restrooms. "Race" was all I heard as Journey dashed to his restroom. It was a game we'd played since he was old enough to walk and was one of my grandfather's long-living traditions. See who could pee and get back fastest. I often wonder if hands get washed during these races. I always do, *of course.*

In the meantime, the line at the gate has grown and passengers are jockeying for boarding positions. I love watching experienced travelers and the uninitiated tourists engage in this ritualistic practice. I sympathize with airline employees and inexperienced travelers as they could certainly feel claustrophobic when this dance repeats itself hundreds of times a day at airports across the world. In some third world airports, the jostling is actually very rude and can become dangerous. In the United Sates it is just a game. Usually, it is started by male passengers, although I have observed female executives initiate, too. First, using one foot, a passenger slides a bag in front of himself. Then, he takes a step toward the bag creating a void between him and other travelers. Sensing an opening, another experienced executive shimmies into the vacuum created by the first, sometimes dragging his bags behind. Frequent flyers lead the human line that worms toward ticket takers.

Inching toward our place in line, I unexpectedly hear my name over the intercom. Perplexed, but beginning to get accustomed to these occurrences, I haltingly walk the fifteen steps toward the counter, moving past other travelers and bags positioned strategically in the aisle. When I arrive, another handsome, uniformed airline official takes my hand. Whispering in my ear while still gazing at the other passengers, he asks Journey and me to follow him. At the front of the line, he displays his name badge and whisks us aboard the airplane. I barely know what is happening, but then, again the entire trip has been like this.

Once again, Deac, Journey's godfather, has ensured our safe passage. I feel figurative daggers pierce my back as we move past the questioning line of envious passengers. I know we'll see them again momentarily, when they board. Embarrassed, I slide down in my seat, hide behind the complimentary blanket and pillow the flight attendant hands me, and pretend to read the safety pamphlet for the fifth time.

First world problem I think, realizing people around the world would love to have to worry about being uncomfortable flying in first class.

"You look like you might need this," the flight attendant says with a wink as she moves back to assist other boarding passengers. The white wine spritzer is exactly what I need at this moment. *Another one of these and I'll sleep the rest of the way.*

"First class again!" I whisper smiling at Journey. As he glances around I see questions developing and know he doesn't understand.

I joked earlier that there is not really first class on the commuters. I remember, like it was yesterday, when Sam explained the same thing on our first puddle jumping flight returning from our Niagara Falls honeymoon. He joked, "Everyone flies *first class* on a puddle jumper." As I learned quickly, back then, everyone also flew *coach* on a puddle jumper.

But the jokes on me now. With the airline mergers over the past decade, serious improvements have been made in amenities. Glancing backwards, I wonder if the other passengers might even get peanuts with their half can of soft drink. Obviously, the airlines have upgraded smaller planes to include first class accommodations so they must be doing something else for the coach customers, too. HA! Journey's perplexed frown softens as the gorgeous flight attendant makes sure he's comfortable, while serving a coke and showing him how to use the in-flight Wi-Fi. We're still on the tarmac, but I think he may have just taken off toward Heaven. She really is cute, *but come on now – Journey, she's ten years older than you. Ten years may as well be a lifetime.*

Our last flight is to Albert Ellis International Airport located in the "metropolis" known as Richlands, North Carolina which is only slightly bigger than Back Swamp. Both of these rural farming towns on the outskirts of Jacksonville, made famous as the home of the elite fighting special operations Marines, are about an hour inland from Emerald Isle. Ellis Airport gets the international designation due to a weekly flight to Canada, although Wilmington and New Bern, larger cities to the south and north, respectively, have daily international flights and accommodate larger aircraft. Aunt Reagan, my mom's younger sister, lives near Albert Ellis and says it will be easier for her to pick us up there.

My excitement is nearly uncontainable. I anxiously look forward to seeing everyone. Certainly the entire family will meet us at baggage claim. I texted Mom and Dad when we landed in Charlotte. Although they didn't respond, I'm sure they're excited too. Cell signals have always been a problem at the coast, and even worse in the Back Swamp area.

First class in smaller aircraft is very tight and I am not a short lady. Flying in a cramped position for fifty minutes, with or without free drinks, makes me appreciate our flight from Los Angeles even more. At five feet nine inches tall, it would have been tougher in coach. *I wonder how passengers in the back of the plane fare.* Unfortunately for them, the lone flight attendant indicated over the intercom early into the flight, "Due to turbulence, there will be no beverage or snack service for the duration of the flight". Ironically she adds not too much later, "Please feel free to walk around the cabin once the pilot turns the seatbelt sign off." *That makes total sense, right? We can walk around on the plane, but she can't? Interesting. Turbulence must not affect the front of the plane as much as the back.* Despite the inequity, I enjoy my drinks and snacks between snoozes in my cramped first class seat.

I grow even more excited as we approach the airport. The lights and landing strip are rising to meet us. I can hardly wait. The pilot perfects a smooth landing and after what seems like another five-hour flight, I'm able to unfold my legs. Rubbing and squeezing, I coax my swollen feet into my shoes. I forgot feet can swell during flight due to inactivity or the pressurized cabin – I'm not sure which is the culprit but the result is the same - pain and more pain. Ugh! When my sneakers are finally tied, I gather my carry-ons and wait for the signal to loosen my seatbelt. I'm glad I'm still almost as limber as I was growing up. I laugh aloud as I hear the clink, clink, clink, as other passengers release their seat belts, ignoring the warning light. At least they stay seated while we taxi back down the runway. I'm sure most flight attendants have given up trying to ensure this safety requirement.

Almost home! I can barely suppress my excitement in returning to the Crystal Coast and my family, not necessarily in that order, of course. Across the aisle, Journey stirs and seems equally anxious. Perhaps this is partly due to needing to use the restroom, again. Of course, he is excited to be moving close to his grandparents, aunts, uncles, and cousins. Finally, he'll get to better know his great grandmother Grams!

"Honey; don't forget to check under your seat and grab your bag from the overhead compartment when we stop."

"You got it Mom. Sleep okay? You drooled a little bit, but your snoring wasn't too loud. Just kidding... It was very loud."

"Seriously?"

"Nah. You were quiet; couldn't hear you over the engine... and no drooling. Are you excited?"

"Yes I am." Using one of Sam's favorite expressions taken from the terrorist tragedy we know as Nine Eleven, I add, "Let's roll."

Descending the retractable steps to the tarmac, I glance at the parking lot. No one there! Security improvements make it difficult for families to meet loved ones as they come off planes. The state of the art, recently completed terminal, also restricts clear vision into the parking lot, possibly for security, too. Surely everyone is hiding inside, waiting to welcome us.

Holding the rail tight - what a shame it would be to travel this far and get hurt on the last few steps - I struggle to check my emotions. Sadly, I reflect, *Sam should be here with us.* I'm sure his mom and dad will be waiting too. If not to see me, then to welcome their grandson home! Maybe even Gram's made the trip to the airport with Mom and Dad. As we cross the tarmac and enter the terminal, again, no one is waiting. Another nine eleven security improvement: only travelers can walk to the gates.

Baggage claim is where they'll be. I'm certain.

We jog the hundred feet to baggage claim, glancing everywhere for signs of family or friends. The terminal is small and no one in sight. Just Aunt Reagan would be nice to see right now.

No one!

Journey asks bewildered, "Where is everyone, Mom? Were we on the wrong flight?"

Confused, I stammer, "Honey, I, I don't know. I mean… We were definitely on the right plane; but I just don't know. Maybe they're outside or perhaps there's been a delay on the road. Let's get our luggage and wait right here." Checking my phone charger plugged into the base-board electrical outlet, I add, "My battery is still dead or I would try them again." Huge tears begin to form, but I can't let Journey see. He reaches out, takes my hand in his, and I give up. They flow like a river. Comforting me with more maturity than I remember him having, he says "It'll be alright Mom. Someone will be here soon."

Chapter 7

Back Swamp

"**M**a'am? Excuse me, ma'am. Are you Kirby Fontaine? Your father sent me to pick you up. I assume this handsome young man is Journey."

Startled to hear my name, I nearly fall off the suitcase I'm sitting on while resting against the support column beside the luggage carrousel.

"That's right. I'm Kirby," I say without really looking up.

All of sudden my mouth opens and a score of questions fly at this unsuspecting man. "Who are you? Where is my family? Why aren't they here? Has there been an accident? Is Grams okay? Is it Dad? Did he fall? What happened?" My mind and mouth are in overdrive from exhaustion and disappointment. Something tragic has to have happened to keep my family from picking us up. At a minimum, Aunt Reagan should be here.

With infuriating calmness, this man I have never met, replies, "Kirby, ma'am, do you mind if I call you Kirby? Everyone's fine. There was no accident and believe me, they are still very excited to see you. It got so late that your dad asked me to run out and pick you up in my truck. He's fine, although he is having a tough time getting around these days. Your grandmother is fine, too. A few of them were headed out here to surprise you with a big welcome home banner, but they had to go to the hospital."

"Hospital? Fine? I don't think so. Who's hurt? Yes, of course you may call me Kirby. Everybody does. It's my name after all. Please take us directly me to the hospital. Can you do that?"

"Yes ma'am. Your grandmother, Grams, I believe you call her--she fainted and your mom thought it best to take her to get checked out at the ER. I'll definitely drive you right to the hospital. May I get your bags first?"

"Oh… yes, of course. Thank you. We're – excuse me, you are correct, this is Journey, my son. We're both pretty tired from the long day. Oh, and I'm never this rude. I've been so unkind when you are just trying to help. I'm so sorry!"

"No need for an apology ma'am, … Kirby. If anyone needs to apologize it will be me when you see the inside of my truck. I sort of live out of it. I can explain that later. At least it will get us to the hospital safe. What do your bags look like?"

"We already have them. I was sitting on this one. They came out quickly since they had first class priority stickers. Not that it matters. I'm sorry again. That sounded snobby. Please don't think I'm rude. We only flew this way because of a dear friend."

"Never crossed my mind."

He reaches down and picks up both bags as I realize how incredibly strong he must be. At the LAX terminal, two men struggled to move my bag. If it wasn't for Deac, I would have paid a $150.00 overweight fee for that one alone. Our new acquaintance picked it up like it was empty.

"Thank you so much. I wasn't sure how we were going to get that bag back to Emerald Isle. With Dad unable to lift much and, well... just thanks!" For some reason I'm stumbling on my words. Lots of emotions are racing, including fear and excitement and, he is pretty good looking and, so far, very charming.

"You're welcome but we need to hurry. I'm double parked out front. If they didn't tow me, yet. Let's get you over to the hospital and then home. I understand it's been a long time coming."

"Thanks again. And yes, it has been a long time coming. By the way, I didn't catch your name, did I?"

"Well, no ma'am, you didn't. I'm sort of working for your dad doing odd jobs and carpentry when he needs an extra hand. I'm not sure your dad would want me to be engaging with you on a first name basis."

"Journey, what do you think about that?"

"Sounds pretty silly to me, Mom."

"Exactly! First of all, I don't plan to be *engaged* with you or anyone else and secondly, you don't know my father very well if you're worried about that. So, what is it? Your name..."

Single-handedly loading the luggage into his well-loved Toyota Tacoma bed he replies, "Well, that's a good question. Since high school, most folks have just called me "ABS". My full name is Alexander Beauregard Boucher. It's French and quite a mouthful. Cajun, if you will. Part of my family moved up here from Louisiana after the Civil War. "ABS" is fine, if you like."

Embarrassed by the feeling that has somehow come over me - my face is probably a bit pinker than it was a few minutes earlier - especially in the presence of my teenage son, I say, "ABS is perfect. Thanks again for picking us up."

I don't mean he's perfect, although I admit he is tall, blonde, handsome, strong, and polite. And the southern accent with, did I hear a hint of the Cajun he mentioned? Might just be my imagination. Hmmm, is there anything else? That can wait. For now, we need to check on Grams and the rest of the family.

"Well, if you're ready, let's roll." ABS says at which point Journey and I do a double take. Journey melts and breaks down.

"What's wrong? Did I say something?" ABS asks cautiously.

"It's okay Mister, I mean ABS, it's just that we lost Journey's dad recently and that was one of his favorite sayings. I said it a few minutes ago and then you said it just now."

"I'm so sorry Journey. I didn't know. And, I'm so sorry for your loss. I've known Sam's family for a long time and heard great things about all of you. Being on the island, you know, there are few secrets. I'm truly sorry."

"It's okay ABS. Just tired I guess," Journey adds as he wipes his sleeve across his cheek and sniffs up the tears remaining near his nose. Shyly smiling, he apologizes for crying like a baby.

"No problem young man. Who's riding shotgun?"

Journey answers, "Mom, you go ahead. I think I'll catch some zzzzs in the back. Okay with you?"

"Absolutely! I'll wake you when we get there."

ABS definitely lives out of his truck -- beer cans are in the bed and last week's McDonalds' wrappers lay on the back seat. Several pieces of wood are stacked near the tail-gate and an old lawn chair is wedged under his tool rack. Most noticeably, however, is the pistol sitting right on the ripped leather front seat.

"Would you mind moving the pistol so I can sit down? I never touch them unless I plan to use them," I whisper to ABS.

"Sure thing, Kirby. I only touch them if I need to. I have a concealed carry permit but I can't bring it into the terminal. You just can't be too careful these days." He lifts it off the seat and carefully secures it in the glove compartment.

"Thanks!" Using the handle, I pull myself into the front seat making sure I don't catch my slacks on the ripped upholstery.

Journey is asleep before we leave the airport parking lot. Heading north out of the airport, ABS turns onto

Highway 111 -- which runs through rural North Carolina eventually turning into Highway 24 --toward the quaint hamlet of Back Swamp. Otherwise known as Freedom Highway, Highway 24 is aptly named because of the two large Marine bases located in the area.

Camp Lejeune, with nearly 50,000 Marines and family members is home to the Second Marine Expeditionary Forces and is one of the largest Marine bases in the world. Its Marines are ready to go anywhere at any time. The New River air wing component, just a few miles down the road, is assigned to the Cherry Point Marine Corps Air Station wing in Havelock, which is about fifty miles north, near New Bern. Sam and I enjoyed being stationed there a long time ago, shortly after he finished pilot training. Altogether, there are nearly one hundred thousand Marines and family members among these three installations. I love their signature saying, "Pardon our noise; it's the sound of freedom!"

It's a bittersweet saying, as I remember the sound of freedom is the reason I'm here - a Marine widow starting over with her fourteen-year-old son. Once again, the tears burn as I keep them from spilling.

Breaking the silence, ABS asks, "Ma'am, I mean Kirby, are you hungry? Thigs Bar-B-Que is right down the road. I can grab some takeout BBQ and sweet tea. They have the best around!"

"That sounds great, but I really need to see Grams and the rest of the family. On second thought, perhaps you haven't eaten. If you want to get something for yourself, that's fine. But Journey's out, and I really couldn't eat right now."

"I'm fine Kirby. I'll get something later. Let's get you to the hospital. By the way, my phone's dead and my charger is cracked or I would call your dad for you. Isn't it funny how these things all seem to happen at the same time? No worries. I'll hurry. If you want to stop I'm sure we can use one of the store phones."

"Thanks ABS. It's okay about the phones. We'll be there soon. Maybe we can get something another time, but not tonight."

Get something another time, I thought to myself? Where did that come from? Okay, he is good looking. But, seriously, I just met him, my Grams is in the hospital, and I am a recent widow!

"Sounds good. Just let me know if you need anything. We're on auto pilot to Onslow Memorial. Should be there in about twenty minutes."

Chapter 8

Grams

*F*inally, there it is. Situated among tall, stately, long leaf pines, Onslow Memorial Hospital sits directly across the street from the Jacksonville Mall. The classic seven story red brick hospital has a large drive-through canopy, typical of hospitals built in the first half of the last century. Located on Western Boulevard, one of the primary thoroughfares in the city which runs right into Camp Lejeune Marine Corps Base, Onslow Memorial provides the best community health care in the region. As tired as I am, and with darkness falling fast, I can still tell that the entrance and grounds have been upgraded since I was last here. They've spent money on curb appeal in the past decade like all competitive health care entities.

I haven't been here since Journey was born prematurely during a prenatal checkup nearly fifteen years ago. Everything worked out fine and I'm forever indebted to the hospital staff. I'm even considering volunteering in the maternity ward to pay them back, now that we'll live nearby. It's rather doubtful I'll ever have another little one, but this way I can help new moms and give back to the hospital and community at the same time.

During my preparation for the move, I researched volunteering here. The nursing director told me she can always use full or part time nurses and she could put me to work as a volunteer in many departments. I guess it's good to be in demand. I noticed on the hospital website The Blue Cross Blue Shield Medical Insurance Association consistently recognizes Onslow Memorial with their highest honor, a Blue Distinction center. We'll see. They can start by providing top quality care for Grams.

ABS slows down and whips into the emergency room parking lot. My pulse is racing as we get closer to Grams. I'm rejuvenated now and don't even feel tired from the trip. Maybe I'm on an adrenaline rush. During the drive, Journey found a comfortable position leaning against some bags and workout gear tossed in the backseat. He looks so comfortable I hate to wake him. I enjoyed seeing some of the familiar scenes ABS pointed out as we drove in. I didn't want to be rude and ask him to stop giving me the tour. He showed me the recently renovated Jacksonville waterfront – but frankly, I'm sitting on the edge of my seat worried about Grams. She just has to be okay! ABS has repeated several times, "she'll be fine." How does he know? Why did they send someone I don't even know to pick us up? I tried to call Dad once more with the little bit of charge my phone got at the terminal. Either the cell signal is still weak out in the Back Swamp boondocks, or no one can answer right now because of Grams.   I kept trying to get through all the way here, but without any luck. Now that we're at the hospital it should only be a few minutes until I can see her and everyone else.

"Journey, sweetheart, wake up. We're here." Journey woke up primed and ready to go.   Hurrying up the sidewalk toward the emergency room entrance, I see Dad and a small entourage approaching us. Aunt Reagan, cousins, and a few guys I don't recognize are in the group. They're strolling – not running – to meet us.

I think about running, but their slow pace worries me. Am I too late?

Once again, tears roll down my cheeks.

"Oh Dad, what's wrong? How's Grams?" I cry, melting into his arms, almost knocking him over. I have to remember Dad still has mobility challenges. After the accident nearly twenty-four years ago, he was fitted with a then-experimental exoskeleton.   Additional treatments have enabled nerve end regeneration, with huge improvements. His dream is to be able to jog again. That is a guarded, but possible prognosis, according to the neurosurgeons. I remember all of this and still have to be careful.

Before he can respond, a crush of girls hugs all three of us while the guys hang back. I hear them all but can't really answer any of them

"Welcome home, Kirby."

"Sorry I couldn't be there for you."

"Look at how tall Journey is."

"Oh My God, he has grown so much."

"Y'all must be tired. Come on, let's get something to eat and drink."

"So sorry we couldn't meet you at the airport…"

It doesn't seem to be letting up when Dad finally says, louder than the others, "Hey Baby, welcome home."

Regaining his balance, he helps separate the small crowd, giving us breathing room. Then, crushing me and Journey with a bear hug only a dad can deliver he quietly adds, "Grams is fine. We had a scare, but she'll be okay. We'll go see her in a little bit."

As the rest of the group waits, Dad looks at ABS and says, "Bud, thanks for picking up my baby girl and grandson." Dad rubs Journey's head with one hand while he shakes ABS' hand with the other, signaling it is time to give us our family privacy. "I owe you big time."

With old fashioned southern respect and good manners, ABS replies, "Mr. Brooks, always my pleasure. I'll drop their bags at the house on my way home and be at work tomorrow morning unless I hear from you. My best to Grams. Sure am glad she'll be okay. Ms. Kirby, Journey, it was nice to meet you. I know you have a lot on your mind. Maybe I'll see you both again once you get settled in?"

"We'd like that. Thanks so much for picking us up. I apologize again for being rude at the airport." For some reason, it's a lot easier to talk with him now. Since I know

Grams will be okay and I am finally back home, I relax. That's it! Or, maybe…, I notice once again how extraordinarily polite and handsome he is.

"No ma'am. My pleasure. Not a problem. Y'all take care. Good night."

"Hey Dad, what's up with ABS and what does he mean about being at work tomorrow? Are you working somewhere other than the fire department? Where's Mom?"

"I can explain all that later, but, for now let's go to the ER. Your mother and Aunt Reagan are there with Grams."

"ER? I thought you said Grams is fine…."

As the rest of the group starts back toward the ER entrance, Dad manages as quick a pace as he can and whispers, "Grams really is fine. She collapsed after helping get your surprise welcome home party organized. You know how stubborn she is and how everything has to be perfect. She is so much like your mom and," smirking adds, "like you too."

"Oh Dad, I am so sorry… and that's not funny! Can't help I get my OCD from them and my ADD from you!" *Man, it already feels good to be home.*

"It was so hot today, especially for May, we thought perhaps she was just dehydrated. It looks like now she may have problems with her kidneys. The ER doc is waiting on a nephrology consult. To be safe, they want her to spend the night. She's out of immediate danger."

Journey seems to understand the gravity of the situation and squeezes my hand a little bit as the sliding doors opens and we walk through the vestibule. Dad ambles around the busy nurses' station as if he owns the place and escorts us directly to Grams. Gently pulling the three-quarter-length privacy curtain aside, I see her laying there, puny and pale, to say the least. Hooked up to several monitors, Grams appears to be resting with her eyes closed, laying under a sheet and warming blanket to keep her comfortable

As Mom hugs me, I melt and whisper, "Mom, it's great to be home."

Journey gets a second squeeze from his great aunt before we switch. Tears well up in her eyes as Mom holds onto Journey. I loosen my grip from Reagan. Finally, we are all back home, or almost…

Mom loved Sam as much as anyone. Here, with her mother lying in the hospital, well, tons of memories are rushing back, reminding her that we're missing a family member. And then there is Pappy. This certainly brings back fresh memories of how suddenly he died.

"I'm so sorry baby girl. I mean about Sam. I'm so glad you're back home where we can take care of you and Journey. But…," she tails off choking on her words.

"Mom," I begin, knowing I had to suck it up and be the strong one for now. "It's okay. We'll be fine and Sam would want us to be here with you today. Let's make sure Grams is okay, and we can worry about other things later."

Where is this inner strength coming from? Normally I, like most adult children, revert to being the child in the relationship even though I'm pushing forty. Is that really possible? I guess it's human nature. I am thankful I can be here for her right now, even though my heart is nearly breaking looking at Grams lying there. Many miserable memories, for sure.

A young, tired-looking doctor, wearing wrinkled green hospital scrubs, slides nearly unnoticed into the room. The on-call nephrologist's name tag reads, Dr. Hal S. Berg. He matter-of-factly examines Grams. She stirs, but does not wake as he reviews her chart and vital signs. "Our patient is going to be fine," he began. "She has not suffered any heart stressors, which was our primary concern. She fainted certainly, but according to the ER report, her circulatory system and neurological functions appear to be normal. Unfortunately, based on initial lab tests, her kidney function does appear to be abnormal."

According to the doctor, there is a distinct possibility Grams will need to begin dialysis in the next few days depending on her lab tests and ability to pass urine. We had heard of dialysis before, but, like most people, are not certain of everything it involves.

His bedside manner is like some of the television doctors, direct while soft and kind. Dr. Berg apparently displays empathy for his patients and shares in layman's terms, that, "Dialysis is simply the removal of bodily toxins or poisons using an artificial kidney and a dialysis machine when a patient's kidneys fail. We used to call it *Dialysis*, as many of dialysis patients would do just that, *DIE*. In our practice, we like to refer to it as *Life*alysis! Lifealysis is **NOT** a death sentence. It is a new way of life. If needed, you'll find that your mother, or grandmother, will be able to resume much of her normal lifestyle. She may be a bit tired sometimes, but, overall, her life won't change much. But let's worry about that in the morning. We'll repeat the tests and decide what course of action to take. For now, she's resting comfortably. Better than all of us, I might add," he said with a wink and smile. "We can all use the same. See you in the morning," he said sliding out of the room.

Only then do I realize it's well after dinner on the east coast. Journey and I lost three hours as we flew back from Los Angeles. I forgot to reset my watch. While I'm beginning to feel it, Journey's face and body really show the strain of starting our trip at four o'clock this morning, nearly twenty hours ago. I lovingly look at his long thin body curled up in the wooden visitor's chair beside Grams. Holding her hand, he is fast asleep too.

Chapter 9

Dr. Gorgeous

"Get out. Get out. GET the hell out! Never! Never! **NEVER!** I will never be hooked up to a damn machine."

Profanity, yelled at a frightened nurse exiting quickly as we try to enter, catches me off guard. Even as a trained nurse, Marine wife, and mother of a teenager, nothing really prepares one to hear or see a sweet elderly grandmother being so rude. Grandmothers hold a revered spot beside angels, or so I thought. At least I'm a bit more coherent than when we arrived to see Grams in the ER last night. After traveling all day and then seeing her looking so pitiful in the hospital bed and gown that made her look like a baby doll, I needed a long rest.

Journey and I slept well upon arriving home from the hospital in the early part of the morning. I barely remember the trip through Swansboro and Cedar Point and I definitely know I slept going over the bridge. I would have remembered that!

I vaguely recollect seeing the huge colorful "Welcome Home" banner stretched across the front of the house. Tables and chairs appeared to be set up for a party in the yard. I'm sure it looked fantastic. Frankly, we were too tired to appreciate it and had more pressing concerns on our minds.

After helping Journey into bed, forgoing tooth brushing or even changing into pajamas, I crashed hard. I haven't been this tired in years! Sam's death and Grams' emergency hospitalization added extra stress. I always need at least eight hours of sleep. Recently, I've been lucky to get three before my mind races back to Sam and what if... But, sleeping in antique twin beds that Grams inherited from her mother, with tightly made twill weave damask sheets and imported duvet cover, reminds me of my teenage visits. Lovely, ... but before I could think another thought I was gone.

Since Grams isn't at Pappy's Place, the family home named after my dearly departed and missed grandfather, and since no one else really has the energy to cook, we settle on a quick bite at the IHOP across from the hospital. I remember hearing about how my birth father loved to eat pancakes at IHOP. It strikes me as a bit odd that we would take time to eat out while not knowing how Grams is doing, but one has to eat.

Dad was ready to go when we woke up, and after a quick shower and change into shorts, blouse and sandals, I woke Journey and made ready to visit. Once Journey is dressed, we join Mom in her Honda Pilot for the return trip to Jacksonville.

My breakfast nearly made a quick return as I realize the profanity I'm hearing is coming from *my* Grams' room. We found the room by checking with the volunteer pink ladies in the hospital lobby. Surely they gave us the wrong number. Orderlies had moved Grams into a private room during the night, which is really good given her current state of mind. I had never heard Grams say anything worse than, "Bless her heart," a comment with multiple potential meanings when coming from a southern lady. Grams may have thought worse, but she never said it in public.

Bravely, yet gingerly, nudging the door open a bit more, I peer in. Grams is sprawled across her bed looking much healthier. Her color is back and she definitely appears ready to leave. "Grams," I said, a bit louder than I mean. After overcoming her initial startle, she reaches out and I bend over to share a gentle hug, careful to not hurt her nor pull out any of the monitoring cables. Journey and Mom are right behind me. Tears of joy streak across her widening smile as Grams clutches fast to my arm with her bonier-than-I-remember fingers.

"Hi Kirby. How's my girl?" she asks, thankfully much softer than the words we heard moments ago. "How was your trip? I'm so glad you made it safely. And Journey, you look so much taller than last time I saw you. Come here and give me a hug."

Journey smiles, leans in - or is pulled in, I'm not sure. Regardless, he loves his great-grandmother and delivers a huge hug while kissing her cheek, causing her to tear up again.

"Hi Grams, I'm glad you're okay. You are, aren't you?"

"Young man, it will take a lot more than a fainting spell to put this old girl down."

This is the Grams I know. Tough as nails, but without the potty mouth.

"Mom," my mother starts. "What's going on? I heard you *speaking* to the nurse as we came up the hall. Has the doctor been in this morning?"

"Oh that. I must apologize to that young lady." Not realizing we had spoken with Dr. Berg before leaving last night, Grams started to tell us of her conversation.

"Jenna," the name she uses for my mother whenever Grams is upset, "the doctor came in before his shift was over. It was well after midnight, and he was tired, but since we were both awake he told me they got the "stat" lab test results back. His partner will be coming in during morning rounds. He wants to talk about starting dialysis. They have some options to discuss with me, but frankly, I'm not interested. I'd rather die than be hooked up to a machine. It's just not human."

"Mom, what specifically did Dr. Berg say?"

"He said the tests show that both my kidneys are not working as well as they should be for some reason. I can still tee-tee a little bit, but not as much as I use to. The nurse suggested that may be why I fainted. Frankly, they said it's good I did. It got me in here before the situation became too serious and I had to start dialysis. Not that thinking about being hooked up to a machine every day is not serious!"

"Okay Mom. Just relax and tell me what else he said. No decisions have been made."

"He also said I might be able to get on the transplant list soon. In the meantime, they want me to start dialysis tonight or tomorrow depending on when the vascular surgeon is available. The dialysis nurse was trying to explain about the quick surgical procedure and dialysis treatments. I'm just not interested. Perhaps when the nephrologist comes in we can discuss options. Phew, I'm tired just thinking about it."

I add, "Well Grams, like Pappy use to say, "There's always a silver lining."" She smiles at the mention of Pappy as I continue, "Just think what might have happened if you had gone much longer without knowing about this situation. During my nursing school, we had a dialysis rotation and another one in the ER. I saw plenty of near-dead dialysis patients come to the hospital because they didn't take care of themselves and some who didn't even know they had kidney failure. Back then, many left being rolled downstairs instead of walking out. That was a long time ago and I believe the treatments are much better and easier on the patients now."

I can see Grams is coming around and beginning to accept this as possibly a good thing. As good as it could be, at least.

"Where's Brooks?" Grams asks, apparently to change the subject. She has always had a knack for easing tension in the room, and she loves her son-n-law.

Mom answers, "He'll be along in a bit. He had to get the crew started and figured you might not even be up yet. He sends his love as always."

Just then, a model-handsome young man enters the room. His name tag, Jody Willoughby, MD is in stark contrast to the Henry James paisley button-down snugged against his biceps and his sport coat carelessly hung over his left shoulder. Someone taught this man to dress. In his Burberry classic leather oxfords, he appears more ready for a date than a dialysis consult.

Grams, Mom and I are absolutely captivated by whatever this handsome physician wants to share. It is probably a good thing Dad's not in the room. At least Grams is paying attention. For the wrong reason, but hanging on every word. Forget she is in her mid-seventies.

After introducing himself and shaking hands with everyone, Dr. Willoughby begins, "Ladies, young man, what we have is a basic case of no-fault kidney failure. Our test results indicate that diet and hereditary are not culprits. I believe there has been no abuse of illegal drugs, correct young lady?" he asks with a wink to Grams who shook her head while gazing, still star struck. "There appear to be no comorbid or related conditions such as diabetes, obesity, or heart failure. And, no recent surgical procedure which can occasionally result in kidney failure. Ma'am, the bottom line is your kidneys decided to simply stop on their own. It happens. Not usually, but not unheard of. So, now we have to decide what to do about this."

"Well young man, what do you recommend?" Grams asks dreamily.

After a lengthy discussion about healthcare options, including hemodialysis or peritoneal dialysis, Grams makes her decision. Grams is extremely active and enjoys her privacy, too. So, she decides on the peritoneal option. The other alternative is to dialyze in one of the nearby "In-center Hemodialysis" clinics four hours a day, three days a week, for the rest of her life. Grams jokingly says the only way that would happen is if "Dr. Gorgeous" provides the daily treatments. He blushes at this comment.

Watching Grams melt, it's clear why this nephrologist was given the consult, especially after Grams' earlier outburst. Grams might have accepted a recommendation to dialyze on the moon given that the doctor is one of the most handsome men any of us have come in contact with in quite some time. The only thing left is to schedule the surgical procedure for later in the day and start the several-weeks-long dialysis training. In the meantime, Grams will visit the nearby "Home" dialysis clinic to be trained and have her treatments, if needed.

At least we have a course of action. Grams is fine and will be released in the next few days. She learned if she is compliant with her physician's orders and completes the dialysis, she could be placed on the kidney transplant list, if needed. It is not likely she will need or get a kidney, but it is better than not being on the list.

After visiting a while longer, Journey and I decide to walk to the hospital canteen and gift shop. In the basement we find the typical vending machines and buy snacks--stale chocolate Moon Pies and Cheerwine soft drinks, staple North Carolina snack foods. Once finished, we head back. What luck. Exiting the elevator as we enter is Dr. "Gorgeous" Willoughby. He exudes charm, and his stylish manner is intoxicating. As our eyes meet, I detect a small smile trying to escape.

One problem! A serious challenge to getting to know this man better might be the person holding his hand. When I see Dr. Gorgeous peck the other man's cheek, I'm pretty sure I heard him whisper, "See ya tonight."

Things sure have changed a lot in this neck of the woods. Even living in a more accepting military environment, I wouldn't have seen that coming, especially so openly. Yep, check this one off the list and I don't think I'll mention it to Grams or Mom, either.

Chapter 10

Pappy's Place

Now that Grams is okay and her dialysis training is planned, I can figure out what we will do for our long term living arrangements. Sure, Journey and I can live for a while with Mom, Dad, and Grams. After my grandfather died unexpectedly, Mom and Dad sold their house at Topsail Beach and moved to Pappy's Place. They have been a Godsend to Grams, but four generations under one roof, even if it is a big beach house, seems a bit much.

We rode back to the beach with Dad so Mom could visit awhile longer with Grams. Dad always knows exactly what to do to cheer me up and he knows my sweet spot! "Candy Edventure" is the coolest candy store in Swansboro and a perfect distraction. Live, finger-snapping music streams from movies like *Willie Wonka and The Chocolate Factory* on the multiple wall-mounted televisions. Ironically, "I Love to Laugh" from the movie, *Mary Poppins* is playing. One of our all-time favorites when I was a kid, we all start laughing as Bert and Uncle

Albert begin to levitate on the screen. Finally, Mary Poppins joins them on the ceiling when they are laughing so hard. Those movies were made when drama, music, and comedy was clean enough for everyone to watch on television or at the theater. And what better way to get us out of our funk! Just standing there laughing allows us to forget about the hospital for a little bit and put us in a better mood. Other than the fact this delectable store is directly across from the town gazebo, where Sam and I first danced at SwanFest twenty plus years ago, my biggest challenge is which candy to select. With more than one hundred different choices -- ice cream, variety soda pops, and caramel popcorn -- I'm almost floating myself. What a great idea to stop here.

Sure, we're worried about Grams, probably more than she is. And I miss Sam constantly. But my family compartmentalizes with the best. Remember, Mom can put things out of her head for fifteen years or more. I'm living proof! "First things first," I can hear Grams saying to help us prioritize.

"Journey, how about some ice cream?" Dad asks while jabbing him in the ribs.

"Absolutely Gramps," hitting him back in the shoulder.

Forget the ice cream. Just seeing my dad and son horsing around makes the stop a success. After deciding on a double scoop of French vanilla and Moose Tracks ice cream, in a waffle cone, while also filling a bag full of gummies for the trip home, we're ready to head to the island.

In a few minutes, as we start to climb the bridge, I lose my appetite.

Sometimes I can't believe I survived crashing Pappy's BMW over the guardrail into the intracoastal waterway. Dad walks with his cane now, because of my stupidity. No one knows for sure how I got out of the stuck seatbelt. I thought Dad cut me free with his pocket knife. Later, I realized Dad broke his back during the sixty-foot jump. He had to be rescued, too, and couldn't have freed me. People eerily speculate that my birth father may have been there to help. I can't really wrap my head around this concept. I ran off the bridge because I had just seen a fifteen-year-old video of his funeral, before I was even born. No way he saved me!

Wide-awake for this crossing, I'm still apprehensive even though I know nothing else *bad* can happen to me. Can it? Dad gently places his right hand on my left knee. Suddenly realizing I'm holding my breath, I silently exhale after we safely make our way onto Emerald Isle.

I'm able to eat my candy.

Dad continues to tour us around the island. He's excited, and it's been a few years since we've really been home for more than a quick visit. Bogue Pier stands exactly as I remember. Why shouldn't it? There hasn't been a major hurricane to hit Bogue Banks in more than twenty-five years. Hurricane Floyd wrecked eastern North Carolina but really didn't do as much damage here as it did inland. As we continue down Emerald Isle Road, I can almost see Sam in the Chowdaheads' window, just like when I jogged from Pappy's Place to catch a glimpse of him. It's a shame the family restaurant closed. Mom and Dad Fontaine had counted on Sam coming home eventually to manage it. It was their legacy. His unexpected and tragic death ripped their hearts out and they lost interest. When I told them I couldn't manage the store, they reluctantly sold to the first buyer. At least they still live nearby on the White Oak River in Cedar Point, so Journey can know his paternal grandparents, too.

Turning back toward Coast Guard Road we pass Emerald Forest, the putt-putt course where I first saw Sam – ummm. Man! Constant reminders – hope it gets easier! This one really hit home. So many memories. I know this will take time. Everywhere I turn and every-one I see will probably remind me of my past.

"Hey Dad, does Mr. Ronnie still own Highway 58 Bikes?" I ask.

"Sure does although he doesn't go in much – Wayne took over, and his kids are helping run the shop. Remember Missy and Brayden? They are all grown up and finished with college. Neither is married, but both are working on it," he smiled looking over his shoulder at Journey.

"Man, that makes me feel really old. Can we head home now? I want to see Pappy's Place in the daylight and maybe take a dip in the pool if it's warm enough. How does that sound Honey?" I asked Journey.

"Good with me," Journey said although he sounded more tired than he had when visiting Grams – it has been a long forty-eight hours.

"You got it baby. Headed home now."

"Thanks Dad. Will you wake us? I think we could use a ten-minute snooze," I said laying my head on his shoulder.

I'm not sure I finished the sentence or if Dad answered me...

We pull into Pappy's Place. Now that I'm awake and the sun is burning off the morning haze, I'm a little sad. Sure, the lawn is green and azaleas are blooming in the flower beds. It's a little early for oleanders and perennials to flower. But, there's something missing. The house and yard just don't have the same punch without Pappy's meticulous daily manicuring and maintenance. Maybe it's been this way ever since he died. Maybe I've been too pre-occupied with life to notice during visits. Then again, we didn't visit as often as I'd like. We were always moving or traveling in support of the Marine Corps' mission.

Certainly, there is work to do in the yard. Strolling around the rest of the mini estate, I notice other areas requiring attention to detail. My balcony - where I would steal naps and spy on people as they walked by our house to The Point - definitely needs to be freshened up. The wood is faded and might have begun to pull away from the wall. I remember what Bob, a golfer friend of ours, once said. "Caulking and painting are like chipping and putting – they both can hide a lot of mistakes." We might need a lot of caulking. With luck, fresh paint will do the job.

Do I hear someone rolling over in his grave? "Yes Pappy, I'm here. We'll help Dad get your house back in shape," I whisper, in case he's listening.

It seems someone is beginning to make some repairs as I notice a pile of two by fours and other construction material on the other side of the pool house. I make a mental note to ask Dad about the lumber.

At least the pool and decking is in good shape and the water's inviting. Nothing like a cool dip on a warm afternoon at the beach.

"Journey, how about a warm-up walk on the beach - all the way to the pier - and then a relaxing swim in the pool?"

"Sounds good Mom. Do we have swimsuits?"

"Good question. We'll figure it out when we get back."

After our four-mile walk we were physically tired but mentally refreshed. The tide was high and the sting of the blowing sand hurt our unprotected skin. It's been a long time since we were here when it was warm enough to stroll on the beach. Today, either the sand is too squishy at the edge of the water as the waves recede under our feet or the sand is too soft and coats our wet feet like sugar covered doughnuts. If Pappy was alive, he would have laughed at our complaining about these kinds of trivialities when other people have so many real challenges. He'd be right of course. However, a serious problem for people living at the beach is not having bathing suits. Journey would be perfectly content to jump right in wearing the old cargo shorts he wore on the flight from LA.

"Journey, we don't have any swimsuits." I remembered during the walk I'd shipped all the summer clothes without thinking. It was still cool in California when I was packing our household goods and I hadn't thought about needing swim suits. "For now, go grab some clean shorts. Race…"

That simple four letter word always brings Journey back to the present. Journey loves to win and knows how important this tradition has been since Pappy initiated it. Even though he is fourteen, Journey still races me to the bathroom, just like he did at the airport. He even wrote a school essay a few years ago about how Pappy started racing me to see who could go to the bathroom fastest, usually when we were out in public. I think that way he didn't have to wait as long. I've continued the racing tradition with Journey although Sam didn't really care for it.

Pappy didn't always win. I remember one particularly humorous story he told about visiting Yellowstone National Park and racing Aunt Reagan. For some reason, Pappy didn't come out for quite some time. Later they learned why.

"I followed an older gentleman into the bathroom. He was upset that the stall was in use so he used his cane to hobble to the urinal beside me. It was a very small bathroom and behind us another man was vigorously washing up in the only sink. Suddenly, my right leg began getting soaked. I stayed in the bathroom until the other two men finished. Then I washed my entire leg in the same sink. I never knew which man it was, or whether I was being washed or peed on!" From then on we referred to this family vacation as the Adventure at *Yellow River* instead of Yellowstone.

In less than five minutes, Journey was poolside and ready to swim. I, on the other hand, was still trying on bathing suits. Mom was still in good shape, but the twenty plus years' difference made her suits a little too big. I never did grow into my tops as my aunt often reminds me. Oh well, the house is protected from all sides. While I don't dare skinny dip anymore, it won't be the first time I've been swimming in panties, and possibly not the last. On the other hand, my Vineyard Vines shorts are too expensive to swim in. With limited options, I'm wearing a pair of navy blue underwear. They looked like swim suit bottoms in the bedroom mirror. The top, however, was another issue. All the bras I packed were white, beige or simply too revealing. Instead, I chose an oversized t-shirt from Dad's chest of drawers... and jumped in.

"Oh My God," I shout, gasping for breath and hurrying to the pool side. I have to get out and get a towel. "Brrr..., It's sooo cold!"

Laughing his head off, Journey is pointing toward the pool house, and, as I suspect we're not alone. I see who he is pointing at as I turn around to climb the last rung of the ladder. Standing beside the pile of lumber stacked by the pool house is a familiar body. Yes, even without the glasses I've started to wear in the past few years I can tell who it is. Yep! It's *him*.

Over six feet tall and not more than ten feet away is ABS. Wearing a goofy grin beginning at one cheek and spreading to the other, he offers me a towel. Obviously, he has seen what I instantly knew - the oversized t-shirt remained on top of the water when I jumped in.

Stammering with embarrassment and shivering I ask, "Why, who, what are you doing here? Who let you in and why are you in my pool?"

"Hang on little lady," he replies calmly. I didn't come out of the pool half-naked. Sorry Journey. No offense to your momma."

"Nope. None taken. I doubted that shirt would stay on. Anyway, I'm not going swimming if the water is that cold. Mom, you coming or staying?"

"I'll be right in, Journey. Ask Grandpa or Grandma to fix some hot chocolate for me, okay?"

As Journey leaves, I hiss, "What are doing here? Are you stalking me?"

"No ma'am. I'm sorry if I surprised you. I believe I mentioned I'm helping your dad with some repairs to the house." Jerking a thumb back at the lumber he adds, "We have a number of projects lined up, so I guess you'll be seeing right much of me." Slyly he adds with a snicker, "That's fair since I've already seen right much of you."

Extremely embarrassed, I am still a woman and conscious enough to notice how he may have gotten his nickname. The ripped, sweaty t-shirt pressed against his stomach and chest suggests he has at least a six pack underneath. As he reaches down and uses the hem to wipe an escaping sweat bead from his brow, I see for sure. There's no mistake. It might even be a twelve pack. This man is cut!

Even still, he caught me half-naked in my pool and I can't let that slide.

Pulling the towel tighter around my body, I growl and turn to leave. "ABS. Don't ever mention this to anyone else and don't hang around when I'm swimming."

"Yes ma'am. Once again, I'm sorry."

"Oh forget it!" I yell over my shoulder realizing how mean I sound when I'm really just embarrassed. "It's Kirby!"

"Yes ma'am, Miss Kirby. Have a good day."

How can he be so polite while being yelled at? This guy is going to be tough to figure out. On the other hand, there is a silver lining. I've been working out, doing yoga, and even jogging a bit. But it sure was cold... Besides, this guy isn't Sam.

Chapter 11

Journey

Changing into shorts and an appropriately fitting t-shirt, I pull an old quilted afghan off the couch and wrap it around my shoulders while settling down at the kitchen bar to sip a cup of hot chocolate. Once I get cold it takes a while for me to warm up. Cocoa is a good start.

"Journey, remember telling me about the hurricane that Captain Crutchfield mentioned?"

"Sure mom. But wouldn't you rather talk about your swimming adventure?"

"Hush your mouth, young man. I'm serious," although my smile sort of gives me away. It's funny, although it would be much funnier if it had happened to someone else.

Looking around the room I whisper, "Never say anything about that. I want to discuss something serious, anyway. The hurricane may make landfall near us in three or four days, depending on its speed. You've never been on the island for a storm like this. There are things we all have to do to get ready."

"Okay Mom. I know, I know. Have cells charged. Tape the windows. Carry furniture and valuables to the highest floor in the house. Buy lots of water and extra food. Gas up the cars, get extra cash, batteries, propane for the grill, matches, and other supplies. Miss anything?"

"Well, aren't you a Mr. Know It All. But I guess you're right. Where did you learn this?"

"I got the storm tracker form at the Food Lion and read it while you were visiting with Grams. Something else I heard this morning on the radio is to put away lawn furniture or other potential projectiles and to not drain the swimming pool."

"You're right, and another thing we have to do is have a communication plan just in case we are separated for any reason before or during the storm."

"Mom, I know you're right, but seriously, it's three days away. Can't it wait a little while? I watched a PBS documentary last night. They said Emerald Isle hasn't been hit by a major hurricane in more than twenty years. Some of the weathermen say it's because the island faces south instead of east. But ya know Mom, I'm not sure hurricanes can tell direction."

"Well, young man, I've been through several huge hurricanes, and we need to be ready, just in case. These are not like the earthquake tremors where we huddled in the hallways in California. Remember, we had an emergency kit for those too. Three days will pass quickly. Soon you'll see lines at the grocery stores for food, water, bread, and other staples.

And, you're right about the gas pumps. The electricity will likely be knocked out and gas can't be pumped. Better to be ahead of all that and ready to evacuate, if necessary."

"Got it Mom. What's our communication plan then?"

"If we get separated, call my cell on the hour and check in. *You* call me so we don't cross circuits calling each other. If you forget or can't call, I'll call you five minutes after the hour. Okay?"

As he answers, Dad walks in. Journey can't resist and yells, "Hey Grandpa, ask Mom about running into ABS again."

"Oh, no! You didn't," I scream with embarrassment.

"Hey Kirby. It's alright. Already heard something about you skinny dipping in the pool. Seems like *you* embarrassed my hired hand."

Punching him in the arm, I reply, "Journey, glad you find a damsel in distress so funny. Dad, it really wasn't anything, but I sure would have liked to know ABS was going to be poolside when I went in with nothing more than panties and one of your t-shirts."

"Ah ha. I believe you jumped in wearing something, but came out without it." Winking, he adds, "And you blame ABS because he was at work during your impromptu wet t-shirt competition?"

"What's a wet t-shirt competition, Grandpa?" Journey asks innocently.

Both of us ignore the question. "Not funny Dad. The water was so cold and the shirt just came off when I jumped in. I swam to the side to get a towel and HE was standing there holding it. Smiling, I might add. Not cool! I'm glad you and Journey think this whole thing is funny."

Hidden a little bit deeper than my raw emotions want to share, I really am happy Journey is laughing. Continuing to share with Dad right now is just about perfect – if *I* wasn't the butt of their humor. Now, for the first time in the past few months, Journey's laughing regularly, instead of brooding. I'm sure Dad is trying hard to help in this area. He knows a thing or two about despair. Just being able to walk up the steps and into the house on his own is nearly a miracle. I worry daily about Journey since Sam died. I too know what it's like. I was young when Pappy died, too.

Journey has such a pleasant laugh – he sounds just like Sam. His impish smile reminds me of when I caught Sam doing something sweet for me. But again, this is wrong; plain wrong. A woman shouldn't have to worry about showing herself, accidentally or on purpose, to someone she doesn't even know.

"Well Baby, ABS has as much right to be there as you. He's helping me repair some of the rotten wood on the deck, the pool house, and even your balcony. I suspect he'll be here for the next several weeks, so my recommendation is to wear decent clothes at all times."

He smiled when he said that. Dad knows I'm as much a prude as anyone and wouldn't purposefully place myself in this type of awkward position.

"How's your cocoa?" Dad asked abruptly changing the subject.

"The only thing that could make it better is some of those small marshmallows Mom puts in it. Where is she anyway?"

"Mom decided to run back down to the hospital. You were busy frolicking in the pool and she knows you need some down time. She'll be back in a little bit." Something just didn't seem right, but I let it pass.

"Okay, well how about the marshmallows?"

"Yeah Grandpa, where are they? I'll get them," Journey quickly chimes in.

"Check the pantry on one of the shelves. You know that is not one of my primary functions. Like Pappy was, I'm an outside dog."

"Got 'em," Journey yelled from the pantry as if he had won the lottery.

It is so refreshing to hear even the smallest positive comment coming from him. I guess I can let the T-shirt go.

Turning his attention to his only grandson, Dad asks, "So Journey, what would you like to do this summer? I understand you were able to finish up ninth grade by home schooling before flying home. So, no school and lots of time. Any idea of what you would like to get into?"

"Not sure right now Grandpa. I know there won't be many kids around here for a few weeks so I thought I might help around the house. Sounds like you and ABS might need a hand. I'm not sure what I can do to help, but I'll try."

"We'll find something for you to do. When I was just about your age, I helped build a deck on the back of a house. I was called the "gofer". You know, *go for this and go for that.* I didn't even know which end of the hammer to use. I remember on the first day being told by the foreman to go to the work van and get a left-handed hammer – I did."

"Seriously Grandpa. You were that clueless?"

"Oh, it was far worse than you can believe. But, by the time we finished I was proud of what I had learned. The master carpenter even gave me the hammer – I still have it. What do you think about helping ABS and me on some of the deck repairs this summer?"

"Sounds like fun. When do we start?

Well, let me check with the supervisors and I'll get back with you. I'll ask Grandma when she gets home, and of course ABS will need to approve as well. Kirby?"

"Sounds like a great opportunity Journey. Who knows, you might even get paid."

"And *you* might even get to know ABS better," he replied with a slight twinkle in his eye. The same one Pappy had.

"Now that this is almost settled, what about fun? Journey, with summer coming what are you interested in? We'll have the cousins up of course and the water park is still here. What would you like to do other than spend all day with me?"

"Grandpa, let me think on that a while. I miss my friends back in California and hopefully one or two might come visit when they finish school. I'm fine to hang out and help you and Grandma. I want to be able to help Grams too. I don't even have a car or a bike so getting around might be a problem."

"Wait just a second. Kirby, are you holding out on Journey?"

"Dad, what have you done? You know better. WE DON'T KEEP SECRETS. REMEMBER WHAT HAPPENED LAST TIME?"

"Come on Journey. Let's go to the garage."

"Oh no," I say. "He's not ready. He didn't even get to take Drivers Ed, with everything that happened."

I remember years ago when *I went to the garage* with Pappy. I was fifteen – an hour later I had learned how to change a tire and check the oil and other fluids. But I hadn't even touched the inside of the car. Hopefully Dad is not doing the same.

"It's not that Kirby. Hold on. We got Journey a home-coming surprise that will solve the issue of getting around, for now."

"Dad. You promised," I whine.

With a chuckle Dad said, "Paraphrasing the immortal baseball great Yogi Berra, "It's *not deja vu* all over again…""

"Huh?" I grunt. I like baseball, but never played, and don't follow it closely. "Why is Yogi Bear playing baseball and what does this have to do with us?"

Ignoring my baseball ignorance Dad replies, "Don't worry baby girl. We'll be careful, and I guarantee Journey won't drive across the bridge." His arm drapes over my shoulder and he plants a tender kiss on my forehead. A feeble attempt to convince me.

It didn't!

In the garage I heard a teen-age whoop followed by, "Grandpa, it's great. I love it. Thanks so much."

Journey quickly put on the matching helmet and jumped on the seat of the new, blue and silver, 50cc 4-stroke, street-legal scooter. "Now there's no problem getting anywhere on the island," he exclaims.

Out of breath after jogging over to the garage to see why Journey was yelling, I say, "Dad, thanks sooo much. You shouldn't have. But wow. Thanks."

"No problem sweetheart. Mom and I picked it up last week. Actually, there are a few miles on it. I just had to see what all the "noise" is about these things. It's fun and makes my getting around the island easier. Might get one myself."

He adds, "Oh yeah, it's tagged, gassed, and the insurance is paid up. After a couple of lessons, Journey will be on his own. No driver's license required. But Journey, you have to obey all the traffic laws and stay on the island. This puppy has a lot of power and can go at least forty-five miles an hour. Promise us you will always wear your helmet. It is not a brain catcher!"

"Absolutely Grandpa; thanks so much. Can we get started now?"

"I don't see why not."

"Now, the first thing you have to be able to do is to change a flat tire."

"I'm out of here," I say, having heard this line from Pappy years ago. "See you guys later."

Chapter 12

Back in the Saddle

The past few weeks flew by. Journey's focus is learning about his scooter and riding around the island. Eventually, there will be more kids when vacationers roll in. Grams is resting at home and thankfully not going to have to start dialysis – at least for now. Her kidneys miraculously started functioning and the doctors are going to try to manage her condition through diet and medicine. As a precaution, her nephrologist had the surgeon install a peritoneal catheter and schedule home dialysis training so Grams can be treated at home if she suffers a relapse and needs to start dialysis. She is thrilled with this option and Mom and Dad can move forward with their home repair projects.

I've finally had time to re-acclimate to "island time" since our homecoming. A few weeks ago we had a small family and friends celebration at The Salt Water Grill in Swansboro. Now that we are officially home and Grams is healthy, I can get out and tend to several much needed personal tasks. "Killing rats," as Grams used to say when

I helped her with chores during my summer visits. Mine are a bit more than that. I need a car and a house. Other than that not too much…

For the first time, I bought a brand new car by myself. That was a really interesting experience. Grams said I did fine. Only once did I almost call Dad.

I wanted a particular sports car and googled it. I compared all the local dealerships' prices, visited the area lots after hours so I didn't have to talk to salesmen, and made up my mind. I went to the car dealership with the best advertised price, wearing my worse looking outfit, as Dad and Pappy always advised. This way, dealers don't know if you have money and won't try to upsell you. The next in line salesman made a bee line to me.

After a condescending and sexist greeting, the salesman asks, "Where's your husband young lady? I usually work with couples or at least like to have the husband here."

I nearly lost it before he could say another word. Shamelessly, I look him in the eye and say, "Mister, my *husband* died protecting my right to buy this car without him – do you want to sell it to *me* or not?"

He almost croaked on the spot. When I wrote a check for the entire amount he was still red and sweating profusely. His Carolina blue shirt was ringing wet and stained under both arms. I hate being mean, but don't make me mad, especially when it involves Sam! As I drove off the lot about an hour later, I waved and gave him my debutante-sweet smile. He probably didn't grasp the meaning.

My cherry red mustang convertible is definitely a ticket magnet. I still drive like a girl although I am trying to drive more aggressively. I guess being taught to drive as a teenager by my grandmother might have been an influence.

Anyway, I'm trying hard to move on. While Journey and I love being back home, we can't stay at Grams' forever and my next venture will be finding a home somewhere on the island.

Today I really need to clear my head. Anniversaries are important, but when it's the sixth month since your one true love died – well, that's a different kind of anniversary. With my eight-cylinder engine feeding my need for speed and my air conditioned leather bucket seats encouraging me to become "one with the car," it's time to explore. Journey's been checking out the island on his new toy while I've been attending to Grams, Mom and Dad.

My turn!

Revving the engine, I turn down familiar Coast Guard Road intending to follow the ocean road through the neighboring beaches. The bike path I used to jog is still there. Much wider and longer now, it meanders well past Indian Beach. Cruising through Salter Path toward Morehead City at the top island speed of forty-five miles per hour, I love feeling the breeze blowing through my hair. I slow down at stoplights and near resorts, where the speed limit changes. I'm enjoying the freedom but for some reason I sense I'm being followed. It's one of those weird feelings. You know, where you just know someone is watching. But then, I am driving this brand new mean machine. Face it -- this candy-apple-red sports car is an eye catcher. *Hopefully, I'm holding up my end, too.*

School's out in some of the states and thousands of tourists have begun their annual migration to downtown Atlantic Beach. I inch along with the rest of the beach traffic to cross the old bridge to Morehead City. *Wonder why this bridge never bothers me?* The road is congested with trucks pulling fishing boats or jet skis and vans jammed with kids heading for a day of fun at the beach.

I wait for the light to change and see to my right the Four Corners Diner which I hadn't noticed before. It's probably been here for fifty years based on the building design. Before I drove away this afternoon, Dad mentioned eating there. "Mom and I ate breakfast there recently. They have great service and the only thing better is the food. If you get hungry stop in. Tell David and Tony I sent you." *Maybe next time. Now I have to feed my shopping need.*

The light changes finally. By pushing the driver in front of me a bit I squeak through on yellow. Heading over the connector, the traffic nearly stalls. Atlantic Beach was nothing compared to this. Then it hits me. Of course. Big Rock, one of the most prestigious fishing tournaments in the world, is this week and of course takes place in Morehead City.

What a moron I am. My family and friends know I don't fish, but I *can* read. I just wasn't thinking when I told everybody I was going shopping. Shopping is the name of the game today, regardless. I'll just have to put up with the jostling crowds and lack of parking places. Journey and I really need swimsuits. I haven't dared take *another* dip in the pool. Never know who might be watching.

After breezing through Island Proper in downtown Beaufort, I quickly check out James Clothing Boutique and Island Outfitters. They have tons of cute suits. But none seem to be me. After hours more of looking I'm near the end of the proverbial rope. I need to find something quick before I head home. Luckily, Tassels in Morehead City has just what I was looking for.   Exhausted after a few more wardrobe changes, I need to head home with my booty. *Interesting word choice*, I smile to myself. I really mean my pirate "treasures". However, the Haley and the Hound swim suits and beach cover ups I snagged may very well accent the other one too.

Stopping for a quick Po Boy Shrimp burger at The Sanitary Restaurant in Morehead is exactly what I need to round out my shopping experience. The tasty shrimp piled inside the soft bun practically melt in my mouth and the endless glasses of sweet tea chase the hushpuppies I inhale. I fondly remember Pappy telling us about the corny potato chip commercial where, "no one could eat just one." He repeated that line every time we ordered The Sanitary hushpuppies. Visitors believe the Sanitary is named because of its cleanliness. It certainly earns that reputation, but old timers and locals know it was named in 1938 when the owners insisted that no beer or wine be sold. Very little has changed. Although restaurateurs up and down the seaboard try to replicate its service and taste, when someone wears a Sanitary Restaurant t-shirt they've eaten the best!

Before lowering the convertible top, I wander across Evans Street into Dee Gees Gifts and Books where I used to shop for hours. Cathy, a long-time family friend, prides herself in offering novelty gifts, beach clothes and accessories, and displaying local and regional authors' books. I always look forward to visiting. The oversized wooden doors open and I feel the air-conditioning, as refreshing as always. The beach music playing takes me back to a more carefree time.

Wow. Glancing at my phone, I realize time has slipped away. Dinner will be late tonight. I promised to help fix it since Grams is still not quite up to par. Sending a quick text, I rev the engine, lower the roof, and put the choppy Bogue Sound water behind me. The warm reddish afternoon sun is beginning to fall on the horizon. I remember the old sailors' belief, "Red sky at night sailors delight; red sky in morning, sailors take warning." Hopefully tomorrow we'll have the predicted good beach weather. Time to drive home.

Drive home…. Home? Now that Sam is gone, what and where is home? Single mom – I get that. Journey will be fine.

I'll make sure of it. But what about me? Wish Mom had been able to join me today so we could talk. I need her, but Grams does too.

What a great afternoon this has been, shopping and carelessly driving around the Crystal Coast. With the top down and my hair pulled tight into a ponytail through my ball cap, I cruise along Highway 24 soaking in the late afternoon rays. Wearing my ponytail pulled through my ball cap – sort of keeps me young -- at heart, at least.

There has been some change on the Crystal Coast over the past few years, but like the ocean's continuously changing tides, much remains the same. The sand and water may be different daily, but in the big picture they appear the same. The blurs of beach houses and condos on the ocean and sound appear to be the same, perhaps updated and painted. But wait a minute. To my left is the most noticeable change in the region. I had heard about, but not seen it from this side of the island. Some people think it is an improvement, while others feel it changes the landscape too much.

The new mid-island connector bridge is higher and wider than the Emerald Isle Langston Bridge and allows twice as many tourists to pour onto the island. Perhaps this is why the Wal-Mart is thriving further down Highway 24 allowing smaller towns like Bogue, Cedar Point, and even Morehead City to grow. I remember Grams talking about the heated town meetings up and down the Bogue Bank townships over the past few years. No one believed it would get approved or built. The Marine Corps giving up their landing strip in Bogue was the icing on top. Not having constant military aircraft buzzing overhead, even if it is "the sound of freedom," didn't upset too many people, especially those who live nearby. I'm sure the government got a ton of money for that waterfront property. I'll try the new bridge later-when someone else drives.

Lost in my memories, I reflect on so many fun times growing up and visiting Emerald Isle with what we call, "The Big Fam-i-ly". Now, I'm the adult with responsibility for building memories with Journey. My mind races as I recall cool places to visit when not relaxing at the beach or pool. I look forward to revisiting The North Carolina Aquarium at Pine Knoll Shores, historic Fort Macon, Shackleford Banks' wild ponies, and the Cape Lookout lighthouse. Then there are other special places to take Journey to like North Carolina's first capital, Tryon Palace, in New Bern, just up Highway 70. Neither of us have been there and Journey doesn't even know his favorite drink, Pepsi, was invented by a New Bern pharmacist. So much to experience – this will be fun.

Six months, today! I can't believe Sam has been gone for six months. December 7th will live in infamy for the rest of the world. For me it will always be the day my life stopped. They weren't even supposed to fly that day. Several of my military friends lost spouses during the past years, some in training accidents and a few in the shortened "Oil War". Each said, "give it six months and then get on with your life." Man, that sounded so cold; however, Mom told me the same thing, and she should know. It's easier to say, than do. Okay I'll try. I'll always love Sam but as of today, I'm back. I know if the situation was reversed he would be an extremely attractive catch and I would not want him just sitting around moping. Well, maybe.

A few days ago and out of the blue, Grams shared an old story about how she fell off a horse at Camp Cheerio. Of course, Grams got back up and went on to ride that horse. I thought perhaps she was having one of her fainting spells or was like political candidates who sometimes forget what they are saying. I figured it out later in the week when I was lamenting my upcoming anniversary. She was telling me if you fall off the horse to get back in the saddle. Okay world, I thought, here I come.

Other than crossing a few bridges offering peeks of the Intracoastal Waterway, Highway 24 doesn't offer quite the same scenery as Emerald Drive, which turns into Salter Path Road and runs all the way to Fort Macon. It is faster, which I need right now. But, I usually love driving along the beach enjoying the island-time pace. Beach traffic, composed mostly of tourists, often called "Tourons" by locals, is exceptionally heavy today. Two abreast, it seems like they intentionally want me to slow down and enjoy life. The pace gets even slower the closer we get to July 4th. Accelerating past the vacationers as soon as I can, I speed back toward the island through Cape Carteret as the wind blows my bottle blonde hair.

I'm super excited and a bit nervous to put on my new Vineyard Vines two piece. I'm sure Mom, Dad, and Journey will give me feedback – asked for or not. I wouldn't mind getting *someone else's* approval too. And Grams, oh my God, no telling what she will say, but, thankfully I've stayed in shape through yoga and jogging and my fast metabolism. My family still calls me the energizer bunny, so we'll see what they say. At least I can wear a two piece – not a bikini; but not a cover up, yet. Journey should like his swimsuits. I found several of the newest, nearly knee length style with surfer themes. Isn't it ironic that boy's one piece suits cover up more body than girls' two pieces? And girl's cost more too.

As I approach the left hand turn to Emerald Isle, I think I see someone waving to me. Carefully turning my head - the steering and accelerator on this beast are super sensitive - I see a dilapidated red work truck pull beside me. Yes. It's ABS. I felt someone has been watching me all day. Was it him?

Waving him off, I punch through the gears and beat him to the bridge. In my rear view mirror I see him putt putting along, sporting the biggest and goofiest smile a man can wear. I haven't figured this guy out, yet.

Chapter 13

Getting to Know Him

Two weeks later, Journey and I have our routines down pat. Grams recently finished her precautionary home dialysis training. Dad and ABS, more the latter, are doing a great job with the house repairs, and I have worked in the yard pruning and replanting -- petunias, vincas and other ornamentals. Grams walked out on the porch after resting inside for almost a month and nearly wept when she viewed Pappy's restored flower beds. Doing this for my family is important and the manual yard work is helping me stay in shape, too. Journey serves as my gofer and lawn boy in addition to helping Dad with the deck repairs. Together we have almost returned the yard to its previous grandeur. Dad was also very appreciative when he saw the end result as he can't get on the ground to do this kind of work anymore. Unfortunately, the folks had gotten comfortable with the status quo, not realizing how bad it appeared.

Transfixed and admiring the results as we put the last bit of peat moss around our new hydrangeas, a soft yet masculine voice behind me asks, "Hey Kirby; how ya doin'?"

"Oh. Hi ABS. I'm fine. Thanks for asking. You?"

"I'm fine. Your Dad's giving me the weekend off. I'm looking forward to some down time. What's going on?"

"Well, we got the yard finished finally. Journey and I were just admiring our fine work, if we do say so."

"And we do say so," adds Journey who has become much more comfortable with ABS than I. Then again, Journey didn't come out of the pool half-naked with a stranger watching. Something like that makes one a little sensitive.

"You really did a nice job, Journey."

"Hey, what am I? Chopped liver?" I ask.

"I'm just kidding. You too, Kirby. It looks great. So, what are you guys going to do this weekend?"

Journey takes this as a cue to leave. He has a sixth sense about giving me space when things might be uncomfortable. Except for telling people about my skinny dipping.

"Well, I'm not sure," trying to buy some time. "Since Grams is better and the yard is finished we might just hang around the pool or take a picnic down to the beach on Saturday. You're welcome to join us."

Whoa. Where did that come from? Did I just say that?

"Well, it's great your Grams is improving since her hospitalization. As far as a picnic on the beach, sounds like fun. Can I let you know tomorrow morning?"

"Absolutely," I say as I secretly wish I could suck the words back in.

Maybe tomorrow he'll say he's busy. I'm just not sure I'm ready for any kind of male companionship, with or without Journey.

"So, been swimming lately? I heard you got some new suits. Maybe I can see one Saturday. The one I saw before was a little revealing."

"Shut up!" My smile let ABS know his joking doesn't really hurt, anymore.

"Well, if you don't mind I'm going to take a quick dip before I head home." He quickly shed his shirt and drops his pants. Thankfully, he wore swimming trunks.

Oh My God! I've seen this man in t-shirts around the house for the past five weeks. Until today I've never seen him this exposed. ABS could easily have been nicknamed washboard, six pack, or any other name that suggests zero body fat with a stomach so tight you can bounce a quarter on it. The Abercrombie and Fitch guys have nothing on this chick magnet. And no farmer's tan. Obviously he stays outside even when not working on our house. I'm not sure what I had expected but it certainly wasn't this.

Embarrassed by my thoughts, I excuse myself adding, "Enjoy the swim. Talk to you soon."

Friday came and went like the previous hurricane, and now the tropical storm will too. Dodging bullets, maybe there's something to this southern facing island thing. It appears to be turning east and should dissipate in the open ocean. We might get some wind and a little bit of rain. "Will probably take thirty minutes to cleanup," according to Grams. "I'll take these kinds of storms all day long," she said when hearing the meteorologist's updated projection.

I'm still uncomfortable with the Saturday beach picnic, but I opened my big mouth. I successfully managed to get word through Dad that we would meet at 10:00 and dodged seeing ABS by volunteering to help Mom run errands in Swansboro and buying supplies at the island grocery store. I also invited Mom, Dad and Grams to the picnic. Curiously, none were available.

I love the beach. Working on a tan, watching tourists play the weekly repeated beach games, and simply unwinding in the warm summer breeze reading a romance novel have always been among my favorite summer pastimes. But today's picnic is an unintended date with potentially unintended consequences. This was not my plan and I need to play it careful. I don't want to hurt anyone. Then again, I did see his abs. If I am going to have a problem, I might as well have something worth talking about. *Talking about…. Right!*

Saturday morning comes so much faster than desired. Right on time, ABS arrives carrying his surfboard and the newest "Zap The Pro" skim board. He ducks into the pool house and comes out wearing bright orange Lacoste swim trunks. I know this brand because I bought Journey the identical suit in Morehead City. Seeing that swimsuit made me remember I felt like I was being watched that entire day. Was it my imagination?

"Hey ABS. I guess I'll go change," Journey yells, as he looks down from the balcony. "I sure don't want people to think we're twins."

"No worries there, Journey. They might think you're Mini-me," I smart up to him, wishing I hadn't.

His eyes and smile show me he knows what I mean even if he, thankfully, keeps his reply to himself.

Watch it Kirby, I remind myself. *It's only been six months and you are not looking for anyone.*

"Whoa. Wait a minute. Hold the phone," I hear which surprises me as Journey yells down at us. He doesn't usually show that much emotion.

"What's up Journey?" ABS asks with feigned surprise.

"You know! Is that the skim board we talked about last week? Mom said no way, too expensive."

"Yes Journey. I got a great deal on it. We'll see how you do. If you can stand up on it, it's yours."

"Down in a flash."

"ABS, you can't do that," I hiss through clenched teeth. I already told him three hundred dollars for a piece of one eighth-inch-thick plywood is way too much."

"Hey, Kirby, relax. I didn't know you told him that. We can work it out and I did get a great deal on it at the new Hot Wax Surf and Paddle Shop. Let's see how he does, okay?"

"Okay, but next time, please check with me before buying something like this."

"I will, but for some reason you've been invisible recently, and I don't have your phone number," ABS added.

Intentionally ignoring the last comment, I pick up the picnic basket and folding lawn chairs and stalk toward the beach. Journey catches us in time to take the board from ABS, who is carrying both boards and hopping through extremely hot sand. Apparently he left his sandals in the car.

Finally getting to an open place on the beach, ABS stops dancing and digs his feet deep into the cooler sand.

"Aaaah," he says cooling his feet. Even ninety-degree sand is better than on top which can cause serious burns. He began to explain his sandals were "stolen" last Saturday morning when he went on his turtle patrol walk.

"I can't believe anyone would want my old Tevas. Worse, I can't believe I forgot to buy new ones. Must be the slave driver I've been helping. No time for myself."

"About that, just curious but how did that come about anyway?" I ask while spreading the blanket.

"Mom, I thought you knew. ABS' grandfather and Pappy were good friends."

"Thanks, Journey. How about you go try out that new skim board you wanted so much while I get lunch ready."

"Got it Mom. I know when I'm not wanted."

"Always wanted, not always needed," I yell after him as he races barefoot through the sand to the surf. With the tide at its lowest, he is soon nearly fifty yards away and focused on his new toy, which is perfect. Close enough to see, but far enough away for us to talk. I really want to hear more about this relationship.

"So ABS, tell me more about our grandfathers."

He went on to explain that they had met when my grandfather, Pappy, moved to the island and needed repair work done on his house. Ironically, it is the same house ABS is helping repair now. As he talks, it is clear ABS loved his grandfather as much as my Mom and I cherished Pappy.

"Pops, as we called him, was a wonderful man. I loved him for his generosity. Pops would give you the shirt of his back if you needed it and often did when it came to helping those in need on the Crystal Coast. He was born in New Bern, in 1922, I think. Plus, or minus a year. He was dirt poor. The butter bean sandwiches southern people love now were all they could afford when he was growing up. And he used to tell me sometimes his mom "forgot" the bread, meaning they just didn't have the money."

"Wow. That must have been tough! Tell me more."

"Well, Pops worked odd jobs starting when he was barely eight-years-old. He delivered the local newspaper when people use to read them. He even worked as a shoe-shine boy for a while on the courthouse steps. He told me once the best job he had as a young boy was being a soda jerk at the original drugstore where Caleb Bradham developed Pepsi. You know the term, jerk, right? The boys used to have to jerk the fountain handle to get the syrup to flow into the glasses. Well, they used to get to drink the extra soda that flowed out of the fountain since they couldn't always get it to stop at the right time. You know, Pepsi wasn't as popular then as it is now. There's even a Pepsi museum right over in New Bern and Pops white coat, with his name faded but still visible in the back of the collar, hangs there with lots of other artifacts. It's pretty neat – sort of like the Coke museum in Atlanta, on a smaller scale."

"Cool."

"It is cool, but what isn't, is why he had to work so young. He had to help his mom, my great grandmother, pay for the rent and groceries. At eight!"

Pausing for a breath, ABS seemed a bit uncomfortable with his next comment.

"Go ahead," I urged.

"Okay. Well, his father, my great grandfather, was a World War I veteran and "forgot" to come back after visiting liberated French women. When he finally *remembered* to return to the states, several years after the war ended, his wife had divorced him, *in abstentia*. When I was little, I vaguely remember hearing my great grandma saying she, "preferred to be free and poor than tied to the yoke of a hooligan." Hooligan was the meanest thing I ever heard her say. Anyway, let me get back on track. The bottom line is my grandfather had to work hard for every nickel he earned and he managed to save a good amount. Pops learned carpentry and metal work repair by helping rebuild some New Bern buildings after the Great Depression. Finally, he became a master craftsman and opened his own shop. I think he even had something to do with rebuilding Tryon Palace. So, when your grandfather was looking for the best carpenter to do some minor work on his beach house, my grandfather was the name given. And the rest is, as they say, history."

"Wow." "So, how did you get hooked up with Dad?"

"That's easy. Fast forward a couple of decades and the story is similar.

"Not too similar I hope."

"Ha ha. Not that way. Anyway, your dad was looking at old house records when he saw my grandfather's name. He had heard my name before from a friend of mine and wondered if I might be in the same business. It happens that I sort of am. Not full time, but for your family, having heard what you all went through, I couldn't say no. I've enjoyed helping, but if we get to something too difficult I'll have to bring in someone with more experience."

"So, tell me about this turtle watching deal; what's that all about? And, did someone really steal your sandals?"

"Apparently they did. So, I left my Tevas, like I always do, by the sign post on the beach when I went on my walk – tell you about the walk in a minute. Anyway, when I came back they were gone. I guess if someone really needs old, beat-up flip flops that bad they can have them. The really good thing about them is they have a built in bottle opener on the bottom which apparently they don't make anymore. At least I can't find any. That was last Saturday, and I really forgot to replace them since I've been working every day at the house."

"I can't believe anyone would want someone else's sandals. That's gross. I hope you have athlete's foot or something else contagious."

"Thanks a lot."

"I mean so they get athlete's foot. So, what do you do on these Saturday morning turtle treks?"

"It's not that big a deal. Nothing important really. Well, actually it can be but so far I haven't really done anything except walk the beach and pick up trash."

"Go on," I urge as it seems like he is holding out.

"Well, okay. You may think it is a bit geekish. Every Saturday morning, between six and seven, I walk or jog a mile section of the beach looking for new sea turtle tracks."

"Mom, Mom, take a look at what I can do…"

Laughingly, I stop Journey, "Hang on Journey. ABS is telling me about this wild adventure he does every Saturday morning hunting prehistoric beasts."

"Okay. Sounds cool. Mind if I listen?"

"Sure. Then we'll watch you. ABS, please continue. Hopefully my rude son will control his manners."

"Well, Journey, I was telling your mom the sea turtles, of which there are seven species, really are prehistoric, just like the dinosaurs. In fact, the Green, Leatherback and Loggerhead's ancestors we find around here date back more than 200 million years. And all of them are endangered! Luckily, many crawl up on our beaches to bury their eggs, which helps regrow the population. Unfortunately, tourists and sometimes even our locals, place turtles at risk when they don't fill in the deep holes they dig on the beach when playing games or pitching umbrellas and canopies. Also, the lights on some of the big beach-front homes can distract or disorient the sea turtles trying to make their way to a safe nesting place. The hatchlings sometimes struggle to know which way to go if the vacation beach houses' lights are on during what we call a boil."

"What's a boil?"

"Good question, Journey. A boil is when turtle hatchlings begin to dig out of their nest, buried a foot or more into the beach, and start their crawl to the ocean. There can be fifty or more of these palm size, perfectly formed baby turtles clawing to get to their natural home, the water. Just think about it. They have been inside an egg for several months, in the dark, and deep in the sand. Finally, they see daylight... The entire mess hurriedly crawl over the top of each other, in a seemingly disoriented fashion, and it can sort of look like the whole mess is boiling. You may have seen the narrow one-foot deep trenches dug near the taped off nests in the dunes. The turtle patrol volunteers dig these a few days before the calculated hatch date so the turtles can safely and more easily navigate to the surf. Otherwise they may go in the wrong direction. You sure you want to hear all of this? I bet I'm boring you both."

"Yes, please. Go on." I say. Journey hungrily agrees.

"Okay. But if I bore you, tell me to stop."

"We promise! Continue."

"Alright. Other challenges turtles encounter include people's trash left on the beach such as bags, soda bottles, children's toys, mesh nets, and other items turtles can swallow or get entangled in. Sometimes they choke on floating grocery bags. In the water, the bags can look like jelly fish which is turtle food. When they try to eat the bag, they can be trapped and drown or become easy prey for other sea life. It's a terrible sight! Then, there are raccoons, dogs, and even human idiots who try to steal eggs. Turtle eggs are considered delicacies and eaten in many places outside the States. But, it's a federal crime to steal them here!"

I never knew someone could be so focused on a subject such as turtles, but it's obvious ABS really cares. My gaze never leaves ABS' eyes as he continues.

"What we do, and there really are many more than me, is get out on the beach before all the visitors so we can locate new turtle crawls. We look for the markings they make with their flippers as they crawl on the beach to nest. The crawls look sort of look like small motorcycle tread, or even your scooter tracks, Journey. We walk along the high tide mark and look toward the dunes because tracks closer to the water in the wet sand would be washed away. We have to get out early. Otherwise, tourists can mess up the tracks by walking in them or accidentally dragging beach gear through them, or disturbing nests without even knowing it. Nests are sometimes even buried high in the dunes where renters of the ocean front homes walk."

"So you're like the Night Watch," referencing the popular Game of Thrones series, Journey quips.

"Ha, ha, I guess we are, sort of, without the magic and the ice wall. Who do you think I would be?"

"I guess you would be John Snow."

"I can handle that. Do you watch it? It's pretty intense."

"Yoo hoo. Over here," I say putting my hand on ABS' chin and pulling it around so he can see me.

"Seriously boys. Can we finish this first? ABS, does this really happen? People leave trash on the beach that harms turtles?"

"Sorry and yes. Absolutely! That's why turtle patrol volunteers walk the entire Bogue Banks beach, from Fort Macon to The Point, every morning from late Spring to late Summer. If we find possible nests or problems on our section of the beach, we fill in the holes, pick up the trash, or call to get the nests marked."

"Have you found any nests this year? I mean with turtle eggs?"

"Nope. Not yet. But one morning I did have three dry crawls, which is fairly uncommon. In fact, that morning the entire island recorded nine crawl sightings. Corny as it sounds, it was exhilarating! I couldn't stop telling people about it. And you know something? They were excited too. Some of the beach walkers even took pictures beside the tracks."

"I'd be excited," Journey adds.

"On the other hand, I went out this morning and came up empty."

Hearing Journey would be excited to do this I ask, "Wow. That sounds really cool. Journey, would you like to go on a turtle hunt?"

"Not a *hunt* Kirby, it's a walk or patrol," ABS laughs.

"Sorry!"

With just a hint of sarcasm I restate, "Journey, would you like to go on a turtle *walk* sometime? I think it would be fun. Although I prefer to walk around nine."

Oh no, there I go again. Back it down Kirby, I remind myself. But this is so cool and who would have thought...?

"Mom, that sounds great. Maybe ABS can schedule a mother turtle to crawl up late one morning, just for you. Now, how about watching me on my skim board. Some of the guys I met down the beach showed me how to launch it in the water and run onto it."

"Great, let's see..." *This is great. He's making friends on the beach.*

Journey really is a natural! Why shouldn't he be? Sam was awesome on any type of board: surf, skim or paddle. I pause, remembering Sam's first attempt to teach me how to paddle board on the White Oak. I got pretty wet my first time, but not because of the teacher. Sam was a patient instructor and I was a focused student. He totally held my attention.

Speaking of attention, let's get back to the present.

"Journey, that's great. You're a natural. We'll get Grandma and Grandpa down here soon so you can show them. Soon you'll be ready to surf! ABS, could you show Journey how?"

Crap, there I go again. And, what is that strange feeling? Suddenly I have a cool chill and the hairs on the back of my neck are standing up.

"Absolutely," he replies adding, "If you can skim, you can surf. We'll do it next time."

Next time?

"So, what happens nest, I mean next?"

"Too funny. You sure you want to hear more?" ABS asked.

"Yes. Please continue."

"Well, once we have a confirmed nest with eggs, more experienced patrol members get involved. They do all sorts of things that I'm getting training in. They record all the "five Ws" who, what, where, when, why... Not sure what the why is. Turtles nest to have young turtles - duh. Anyway, they record all these statistics so they can track where the mother has been before and how many times she has nested there. Maybe that's the why, come to think of it. They also take a DNA sampling of one egg to determine its ancestry.

"Seriously?" I joke.

"No, really! It gets more detailed too. They record the actual GPS coordinates of the nest, stake it out, and put colorful tape around the stakes to remind people to stay off. After that we sit back and wait. Anywhere from fifty to seventy days or so, depending on the species, the new turtles arrive. Just before the expected hatch date, the patrol gets involved again, trenching out the path I mentioned earlier which helps hatchlings reach the surf. They usually hatch later in the evening, supposedly when it is cooler and predators are not as active. I'm not sure the turtles actually know what's going on above them when they are buried so deep. Anyway, the patrol tries to watch the nests in the evenings and keep people from bothering them. Plus, during the day there are usually lots of people on the beach to help watch the nests."

"Wow, I guess I've been too busy with my family and friends to pay attention to how important turtle protection is. I remember seeing the stakes, but I never knew what they were."

"Kirby, don't beat yourself up too much. Most people don't know. They come here to enjoy the beach and relax. And truthfully, the turtle patrol program has become more well-known now that we have the North Carolina aquarium in Pine Knoll Shores. Their emphasis on protecting all of the coastal environment and improving marine education has really helped. Have you been?"

"Not in a really long time. Maybe Journey and I will go sometime." Phew, dodged the question this time.

"Now that I know everything I ever wanted to know about turtle watching, how about some food?" I joke.

"Lead the way. I'm famished."

After a scrumptious picnic, which we protected from a flock of vulture-like seagulls, I was ready to work on my tan. ABS and Journey had other plans. They seemed like best friends playing in the surf. Journey is getting pretty good on the skim board and ABS showed him a couple of tricks. I thought perhaps smaller or skinny boys could skim better. ABS is big and muscular and did all the same tricks, too. Easy on the eyes, it was difficult to not appear interested in ABS.   Enjoying the beach with this tanned, toned, and easy going man, with a mane of hair Zac Efron would covet; seriously, what's a girl to do? But, come on, he's almost ten years younger than me. Well, okay, only eight but I could have been his baby sitter.

"Phew, I've been sitting for a while. How about we walk off our lunch?"

"Let's do it," ABS replies, as he finishes toweling off his chest and hair.

"J, we'll be back in a little bit." Journey ignores or doesn't hear me as we stroll away.

Walking in silence toward the pier is comfortable, yet uncomfortable. To break the silence, I ask, "So tell me about helping my dad and Grams. You mentioned our grandfathers, but what's the back story?"

"Great question. Last year, while we were hanging around the "E" Club, some friends were talking about a rich old lady and her daughter in need of a carpenter to do repair work on their home. No one wanted to touch it because of the reputation that everything has to be perfect for this lady. When I found out whose house it was, I jumped at the chance to help. I had heard the story about your dad, and frankly, what happened to him on the bridge. And we all know Pappy's reputation. He was a living legend around the island. Finally, the fact that my grandfather had worked on Pappy's Place a long time ago sealed the deal. When I met with Grams, I fell in love. She's a dear, and your mom and dad are great too. Not sure what the issue was with my friends, but they missed out. I'm glad your dad was looking for someone and I was available."

"In more ways than one," he adds with what I think is a wink.

Maybe a little sunscreen or salt in his eye?

"Let me get this right. The rich old lady is Grams? And your grandfather worked on my house, or really my Grams' house?"

"Sure did. Like I mentioned earlier, he was a master craftsman and had such a reputation he became much more on the island. He was an astute early investor and builder on Emerald Isle, along with a few other guys back in the late 50s and 60s. His buddies, Ronnie Finch, who owns the Holiday Trav-L-Park and was the first Emerald Isle mayor, his long-time friend Matthew Johnson, and a few of the original investors like Jeremy McLean were responsible for building some of the really nice developments and houses on the island. But that's another story. My grandfather was well known for building up and down the Crystal Coast. I like to think I inherited a little of his talent. Anyway, when I got to Pappy's Place, it really did need some interior work and the decking definitely needed replaced. Recent deck failings scared Grams, especially with more and more of the family visiting. So, I've been working with your dad since shortly before you arrived. I love seeing how my Pops used his craft on your family home – no way it will ever come down, even in a Category Five hurricane. Most of my repairs are cosmetic. Only the health suite, as Grams now refers to it, is new. Since we were enlarging her bedroom anyway, we've modified a portion of it into a "clean room" with enough supply storage and space for her home dialysis machine. Hopefully she won't need it."

"Wow. I've watched as you and Dad were working, but had no idea of everything you're doing. Grams showed me her new room. It looks great."

"Well, we're almost finished, and none too soon. I hear there is another hurricane brewing. It's a tropical depression right now. There's a good chance it won't come this way, but you never know. It's good to have a hurricane kit already prepared. We call it a "bug out kit" so we are ready to bug out. I know that's an old saying, but it works."

"I know the term. Sam, like many military guys, always had a kit ready. Dad probably has one in his car, too."

"Well, I don't like having all the loose lumber and supplies laying around. The house will be fine, but I need to put that away soon so the boards don't become missiles."

We sidestep hordes of people crowding the public beach access and splash through the incoming tide, covering our feet with sand.

ABS surprises me when he says, "Man, your feet look good enough to eat."

"Huh?" I grunt. "Want to explain that?"

"Sure, they look like powdered sugar doughnuts and I love doughnuts."

"Okay. Never heard that and it just sounded a bit weird." Back to walking in silence, although this time I knew why. That was certainly an interesting comment.

Time flies as we finish walking and return to "our" beach. Man, I sure am glad we don't fight for beach space like those who use the community accesses or stay at the nearby condos. It's funny how a few hundred yards in either direction can make such a difference. It's hard to complain about not having enough space while walking on a stretch of heaven.

"ABS, I really had a great time today. Thanks for the walk."

"Me too, Kirby. I sort of feel like I monopolized your time and the conversation. Thanks for the lunch. It was second only to the company. Maybe we can do it again."

"Maybe," I said. "I'm just not sure if I'm quite ready."

"I understand. Well, thanks again. I had fun too and I enjoy just talking with you."

Journey jogs up from the water just in time, helping clear the tension.

"Hey ABS, thanks again for the board. Some of the guys showed me how to jump the wake – I'll show you next time."

"I saw you Journey. You did great, and I'll take you up on that offer next time."

"Awesome. Let me know when I can turtle walk with you."

"I will." Hurriedly he adds, "I have to run. See you soon. Bye Kirby, Bye Journey."

"Bye ABS," I say more forlornly than intended.

Chapter 14

Mother Knows Best

"**M**om, I just don't know about this. Sam's barely been gone six months. For Heaven's sake, the memorial ceremony is Sunday."

…

"Well, of course I enjoy his company. He's a great conversationalist. He listens to me and takes time answering. He looks in my eyes and gives me a chance to make my point, without stupid sexist comments like other guys might. That's important today, when people say and do as they please. But what will people think?"

…

"Who cares? I do, for starters."

…

"Seriously? People have already said that? They think ABS and I would be a good match? How funny is that, since we haven't even dated."

…

"No. Going to the beach wasn't really a date. Remember, Journey was there too. All we did was talk, eat lunch, lay out and take a long walk to the pier and back." *Hmmm. Maybe...*

...

"Okay, okay. I know... I need to move on. And yes, no one is pushing me, although it feels like you might be starting. But Mom, there is something weird going on. I still feel as if I am being watched and sometimes I think it might be ABS."

...

"Possibly. But you know I haven't had these kinds of premonitions since the bridge episode. I've heard of other people having them. Even Stephen King wrote about them in his book, Dr. Sleep. He calls it, *"the shinings."*

...

"I don't know. Just feels weird. And thinking I have someone following me is creepy."

...

"Okay, I promise. I'll keep an open mind and yes, I know everyone knows I loved Sam. I *STILL* love Sam! Do you think I'll ever get over him?"

...

"Thanks for taking my call. I know I can be annoying. I was just driving by the private cemetery up Highway 58 and well, you know... I just needed to talk."

My tears had dried up in the last few minutes but begin to flow again as I choke out, "Thanks Mom. I'll be coming home after we finish looking at the Salter Path cottage we're considering. You know the one. It has the teal

Bahama shutters on the sides. And, the lift so Dad can get to all the floors."

...

"Yeah, that's it. Right on the ocean. Not too far from the Doubletree hotel. I'll be back by lunch. Love you. Bye."

Great moms are so underrated. She's earned every penny I spent on her Mother's Day plaque that reads, "God couldn't be everywhere so he made Mothers!"

I haven't had a breakdown like this in several months. Sure, they come and go and minute by minute I can cry my eyes out. I never know what will trigger it. This time, the Tom Odell version of "Grow Old with Me" playing on the radio nearly stopped my heart. I hadn't heard it in years. Luckily, I had already started to slow down and pull over to listen. It hit me harder than I imagined it could. My head felt like exploding with what seemed like the beginning of a migraine. I was totally disoriented. My equilibrium was way off and the flashing lights I saw, even with my eyes closed tight, were better than the blue police or amber emergency lights I might have otherwise seen. I might have killed someone if I'd kept driving. The red truck blowing its horn was a life saver.

Wait a minute. Red truck? ABS has a red truck. I wonder….

Chapter 15

Get Over It

I'm exhausted! Coordinating Sam's Memorial ceremony this Sunday at the Holiday Trav-L-Park has been my first priority. It has to be perfect. Low-key, but perfect! When he grew up, and even when we visited Emerald Isle during military leaves, Sam attended the non-denominational service Ronnie has provided for campers and locals for nearly forty years. Ronnie enthusiastically thanked me for asking him to host the service in his park. He even insisted on having one of his favorite groups, who regularly play at the Sunday church services, sing Sam's favorite songs.

One down, two to go.

Finding a new home for Journey and me is second on my list. Journey and l agree we want a three or four-bedroom condo or beach house with limited yard work and beach front or at least a beach view. We've looked at several and narrowed it down to the Salter Path cottage. We've been spoiled living on military bases, where in recent years the bases have started mowing and edging the housing area yards. We definitely want to enjoy our home and not have to work in the yard. Staying at Pappy's Place convinced us of that. We don't want to live at the beach and think about mowing a yard or planting another flower.

Our first choice is the beautiful beachfront four-bedroom cottage. Like I told Mom, it has a lift which will make it easier for weekly grocery trips; Dad can use it; and we can use it to move our furniture. The beautiful teal Bahama shutters provide the beachy colors I want, without the flowers. And the ocean views from each of the decks are breathtaking. While I can't ogle people coming and going like at Pappy's Place, we will certainly be able to watch sunbathers and surfers, without leaving our house. Perfect! And, its only about thirteen miles up the island. We'll be able to get to Grams' in twenty minutes. Once I check out the traffic situation, Journey might even be able to ride there on his scooter. I put in an offer and will know soon. Dad will probably be upset that he didn't see it prior, but I have to do things on my own, eventually.

Two down, one to go.

Oh man. I've avoided this for the past three days. Each time ABS calls, I don't answer. I just let it go to voice mail so I can listen later. I learned that trick a long time ago. I just haven't been able to call him back. I'm not sure what to say. His last message was so sweet. ABS thanked me for a beautiful time on the beach and said how much he really enjoyed helping Journey with his skim board. It was a perfect message until…. until he asked if I would be interested in going out. There is still something in the back of my mind that continues to nag me. The red truck, or one like it, was there when I had my emotional break down and called Mom. It seems to be everywhere. But I'm not positive it is his.

That last call precipitated my second urgent call to Mom this week. In fact, I was way too emotional and had to wait an hour before I could call. How can I consider going out with someone when my husband's memorial ceremony is in a few days?

Mom was not very helpful, which is so unlike her. She reminded me of our last conversation about the same subject and sharply said, "Kirby, get over it." I can still hear her words, "Sam would want you to be happy **and you know it**!"

Ouch. Journey echoed that sentiment, although I could tell it pains him to think of me dating. It's clear he likes ABS. He has from the minute we met at the airport.

Third chore: *Okay*, I tell myself. I'm calling, **now**.

"Hi ABS, it's Kirby. How are you?"

"Hi Kirby, I thought I made you mad or maybe your phone was broken again." I think I detect a little humor in the last part.

"Ha! I just needed some time before I called you back."

"That bad? Really"

"No silly, not at all. I love your messages. It's just that Sam's memorial is this weekend, and I've been in a funk. I haven't considered dating - anyone. Mom convinced me I need to reconsider. So, we have two things to think about: what the future holds and do you realize how old I will be when you are forty?"

"First, your mom is a smart lady. I believe in the saying; *Apples don't fall far from the tree.* Another saying a close friend of mine told me once is, *Age is just a number.*"

"Is that close friend an older woman?"

"Good try! Kirby, sometimes life gives you second chances and you have to grab hold of them. No one is ever given a sure thing. I'm not even guaranteed to make forty. What I do know is we are both here for some reason and I want to get to know you better. So, how's Tryon Palace next Monday?"

Gulping, I said with my sweetest voice possible, "I think that will be okay." How bad can it be in a palace? "But what about the hurricane?"

"Rain check, if necessary. Otherwise, I'll pick you up Monday at Grams' about 9:00. I don't think this hurricane is going to be bad, maybe some wind and rain. It really isn't expected to make landfall, but there is a tropical depression named Michele brewing. We'll keep watching for that one in a few weeks or so."

"Okay then. I'll make sure Journey can stay with Mom and Dad."

Well, that wasn't too bad. I've just about made it back to Grams. I guess I need to take a look at my closet and see what I can wear.

One thing still bothers me. Someone is constantly watching me or listening to my conversations. I was just talking with ABS, so I guess Mom is probably right about him. Then, who?

Chapter 16

The Send Off

Sam's memorial, conducted at Edwards Air Force Base in conjunction with the Marine Corps, was typical military -- ostentatious compared to our low-key Emerald Isle plans. Sam would have been displeased with all the fuss. They had their turn. Now it's ours. We really want it to be like Sam would have liked!

Finally, all my family is gathered to support us as we say goodbye. Only Mom and Reagan and, of course, Sam's parents, flew to California for the service six months ago. Nearly one hundred friends join us this beautiful summer morning to help send Sam off, one last time.

Using the Trav-L-Park outdoor cabana for the by-invitation intimate service is perfect. Certainly it's not very private in the middle of a travel park, but it is exactly how Sam would have wanted. Born on Emerald Isle, he'll soon to be resting forever in the nearby waters of the Atlantic, surfing every day like he planned to do, when we finally retired. Ronnie's daughter, Tammy, helped Mom and Grams plan the ceremony including the eulogy, music, and even helped select the floral arrangements. The beautifully draped red, white, and blue streamers at each of the entrances afford us as much privacy as possible in this rustic outdoor campground setting. Flags representing each of the armed services are uniformly and crisply arranged behind the makeshift altar, providing just the right degree of respect for the military as we close out this chapter of our lives. Multiple unknowing campers and guests wander by, wondering what's happening. The staff keep most of them at bay.

True to his word, Ronnie secured one of Sam's favorite gospel quartets. Curtis Hyler and his quartet, Jubilation, have provided summer-time, non-denominational services at the travel park resort for decades. Each of the members drove several hours, from their eastern North Carolina towns, out of devotion to Ronnie and respect for Sam. Country through and through, Sam was true to his roots and always stopped in to attend a morning gospel service when we visited Emerald Isle. Now he'll be close enough to attend every Sunday.

Once again helping us through this ordeal are good friends, Deac and Sally. They flew in a few nights ago from Japan where Deac had asked to be reassigned following Sam's death. He desired to get far away and to not be reminded of his buddie's death daily. I can't blame him! Bunking in our spare bedroom over the garage, they are a Godsend! And of course Reagan and the rest of the family have been so helpful.

As the United States Marine Corps hymn plays quietly, Deac leads sandal and shorts wearing ceremonial pallbearers to the front. Sam is already at the altar in his ten-inch urn sitting patiently beside a picture of the three of us on our last Hawaiian vacation. Ronnie opens with a prayer and chokes out his welcome. Jubilation follows a cappella and reopen my tear ducts singing Brad Paisley's, "When I Get Where I'm Going."

The usual morning campground activity drowns out much of the sniffling and quiet crying beginning to spread throughout the packed pews. Sam's dad stands and shuffles to the front to offer his painful eulogy, one a father should never have to give. Valiantly beginning, his hands shake as he grasps the podium. The loss of his only child has shaken this once strong man to the core. He's aged ten years in the past six months and can't finish.

Feeling the loss, Dad looks at his friend and struggles to rise. Dad ambles to the altar and clasps his loving arms around Sam's father. Together they remember briefly what Sam means to all of us as Dad says,

"Father, husband, son, friend, and military hero. Sam loved Kirby with all his heart and treasured his only child, Journey. He was the most respectful son and always loved his momma and dad. Sam was also an Emerald Isle favorite son. My wife and..."

Now Dad chokes back his tears. Before continuing, he gulps in a breath of the fresh air stirring from large rotating overhead fans.

"... and I. We loved Sam Fontaine. Always will. I couldn't have asked for a better son-in-law. From the moment Sam drove down Pappy's driveway more than twenty years ago in his beat up red Volkswagen... Well, Grams and Pappy couldn't stop talking about this charming young man. And, you know, they were right. Many of you may remember Kirby's grandfather, Pappy. He reminded us often with the story of how Sam brought Kirby home after she fell running to the pier... to check him out. *They* knew what she was doing - it was fate that made her fall." That broke the ice, with a spattering of laughter.

"Well... like his mom and dad, we knew he was a keeper. And so did she! We never would we have expected this. But, Sam knew the risks and made all the provisions. He and I shared intimate talks about the possibilities of his being hurt or killed. And, well, he was. But, he died doing what he loved. Today we don't say goodbye. We say until we meet again."

Sam would have hated a big deal being made about him and I aim to be faithful to his wishes. I made certain there is no tear-jerking American flag presentation this time. Been there - done that! No widow should ever have to do that, twice. But, I can't stop his mom from crying and sniffling. It's been almost six months and his mother's tears flow like a river. I understand.

After comments from a few family members, Dad stands again and says, "After the singing of our last hymn please join the family on the beach. We have golf carts to help any who need help walking there."

Jubilation begins, "Amazing Grace, how sweet the sound…" I'm not sure I get this *amazing grace* thing. Here's the personal thoughts that race through my mind as the congregation softly sing this favorite funeral folk song:

Father survives Afghanistan - is shot and killed in his neighborhood, before I even knew him.
Husband survives a war as an ace fighter pilot - dies ditching an experimental jet in the Pacific.
I need to see some of that Grace pretty soon.

Gathering my composure, arm-in-arm Journey and I join the rest of the caravan for the walk to the beach. The temperature is soaring. It must be close to ninety degrees already. My blouse sticks to my back. Wearing my hair short, like when I first met Sam, makes a big difference at the beach. At least it doesn't frizz out like Bozo or Ronald McDonald. The funeral party has swelled to several hundred by the time we arrive with Sam's parents, who are struggling more than when they were in California. Perhaps shock helped get them through last time. Thankfully, the ocean's high tide makes the walk to the water's edge shorter and much easier for Dad and other *differently-abled people* struggling to maneuver through the sand.

It seems like everyone on the island knows about our ceremony and is here to pay respect. Many of the new arrivals wear bathing suits, cover-ups, or shorts. The only thing missing is beer although it may very well be in their cups.

Sam would love this, maybe even laugh, if it wasn't so sad. Eventually, the semi-circled crowd presses forward until my feet are getting wet. I'm actually sinking in the sand as the waves lap across my ankles. Without fanfare and knowing we can't stay out here too long, I take the urn and trying not to splash everyone, move in front of the closest relatives.

Looking upward and away from the crowd's gazes, I choke out, "Friends and family, Sam loved the beach as much as anyone. Today, we return him from whence he came. Every day, he'll be enjoying the ocean breezes. And now, y'all can visit whenever you want. Journey and I thank you so much for coming. We love you."

To complete the ceremony, I pour a handful of ashes into Journey's hands. I can't look him in the face or I'll fall apart. Next, I share with Sam's parents, both trembling as if freezing. Finally, I pour ashes into my parent's hands and take the rest in mine.

Nodding, together we reach down and allow the water to flow through our hands and between our feet as Sam returns to the island and water he cherishes. As quickly as it began, we finish.

The crowd dissipates like a flock of seagulls chased by a child. Short-term memory is alive during the summer at the beach. I don't blame them.

As family and close friends talk about going back to Pappy's, I say, "Journey and I are going to walk home on the beach."

"You sure baby?" Dad asks.

"Need alone time," I choke out, waving as we turn to walk away.

As we begin, I ask, "Journey, Honey, wait just a minute. Who is that standing in the back near the sea wall?"

"Where Mom?"

"Right up there." As I glance back to point, he's gone.

Maybe it's my imagination. I swear there was a man in a pilot uniform standing in the background looking our way. He looked so familiar. Not wanting to freak out Journey I say, "Never mind. My mistake. Come on kiddo, let's roll." I get the desired smile with the last comment as Journey reaches over and takes my hand. *Never too old to hold Mom's hand – I hope.*

"Holy cow, it's hot," Journey exclaims, walking toward the beach house and wiping sweat from his forehead.

"Sure is! Luckily we only have about a mile more."

Lucky, also, none of the beach goers have asked if they can help. We must look pretty scary with my mascara smeared, tear stained cheeks, and both of our outfits clinging to our bodies from the surf and sweat. But down time is exactly what we need.

As we approach our beach access, a lone figure stands waving at us. This time I realize who I had seen after the ceremony. It's Crutch or rather, Captain Crutchfield.

Looking in that direction Journey asks bewilderedly, "Mom, is that Captain Crutchfield?"

"I think it is. Not sure how he knew about today. Did he ever talk to you about the service?"

"Nope. I haven't talked with him since we flew home."

"Me neither. Sort of strange, don't you think?"

"Well sort of. He did fly with Dad so maybe he heard about it from friends or on-line."

As we near him, I whisper, "You're probably right. Just a weird feeling. And for sure I never told him where Pappy's Place is."

Before Journey could respond I hear, "Hi Kirby, Journey. It's me, Crutch. Hope I'm not intruding. I wanted to say hello at the beach, but you were gone in a flash."

I really wasn't, I thought, but let's give him a chance. Carefully I respond, "Surprised to see you Crutch. How did you find me -- I mean, us?"

"Mom, I'm running ahead. I'll see if Grams, Mom, or ABS needs any help."

Smart boy.

He adds "ABS" to let me know they'll be watching in case anything weird happens. *Sam*, I thought, *you raised a nice young man to watch over his mom.*

"Okay, I'll be right there. Please tell ABS I'm on the way, if he needs me." Another subliminal message, just in case.

"Good to see you Journey. See you later."

"You too. Bye Captain Crutchfield."

"Kirby, I know this is a tough day, and I want to be respectful. Truth is, I've been thinking about you very day since we met. I can't get you out of my mind."

"Seriously? TODAY is not the day! Of all days, how can you even think about saying something like that?"

"I'm sorry. I really don't want to upset you. I just hope you'll let me explain why I came to the service."

"Sure. You have two minutes – go!"

"Thanks," he said with a pace and tone indicating he knows I'm upset. "I'll hurry."

"So, I saw a Facebook post about the memorial service and, well, I changed my flight schedule so I could dead-head to Wilmington. Just made it and I have to go right back to catch my return flight. I fly my California legs tomorrow."

If he thinks I'll be impressed, he is surely mistaken. "Go on."

Seeing Crutch sweating like a pig in his white and black pilot uniform, I could almost feel sorry for him. I know how hot it is on the beach today. I just walked two miles with the sun burning down on me. And, I'm not wearing a suit, patent leather shoes, and a cap. He must be so uncomfortable. Any empathy I may have had evaporated when he added, "I just needed to see you again."

"So, are you here for Sam, Journey, or me? I'm confused," I said in a decidedly snotty and increasingly hostile tone.

"Hey Kirby, you okay? Afternoon Captain. Can I help you?" ABS had obviously gotten the message and found me. He had changed out of his memorial outfit and was wearing his swimsuit, minus the shirt. Intentionally, I'm sure.

"No ABS. No problem. Captain Crutchfield was just paying his respect. He flew with Sam during the war. He's leaving now. Aren't you Crutch?"

"As you wish Kirby. Please think about what I said."

Walking past ABS, he asked, "SEAL Team 3?"

Placing his arm round my waist I heard ABS grunt, "Hooyah," which means "yes" in Navy Seal talk. I learned during our military career, every organization has variations of this word. It means different things depending on inflection and when it is said. What I had not learned before was about ABS and Seal Team 3.

Note to self. Ask ABS about Seal Team 3.

Now that Captain Crutchfield has been dispatched through ABS' able body and timely assistance, we walk up the path to the house. I know I'm in the right place at the right time. Sam is finally at rest and I can now move forward.

Chapter 17

Tryon Palace Secrets

In his beat up pickup truck, ABS rumbles down our driveway, not unlike Sam did more than twenty years ago. Mom had a thing for Marines and firemen. Maybe I have a thing for guys with old beat up vehicles.

Back in the saddle Grams? Really? This still feels wrong, although I would hate for ABS to know what I was thinking.

"Hey Kirby, you sure you want to go? Looks like your face got stuck sucking a lemon. Either that or I forgot to shave or bathe. Did I?" he asks jokingly, as he pretends to sniff under his arms.

"Oh ABS, I'm sorry. It's not you. You know what I've been going through. I'm excited about today. It just feels a little weird. Will you come in and say hi to Grams? She's been wanting to talk to you since you finished the repairs. I think she's thinking of more repairs to keep you around." With a hint of comedic relief, I sing song a parody of Sandra Bullock's line in Miss Congeniality, "She thinks your gorgeous; she wants to date you."

"At least *someone* likes me."

"Ouch. I like you. Well, you know. You're practically ten years younger than me – I could have babysat you."

"That would have been awesome! Every boy's dream. Come on YOUNG lady. Let's go see Grams."

Always the southern gentleman, ABS answers Grams politely, "Yes ma'am, Grams. Of course we'll be safe. What could possibly happen between here and Tryon Palace?"

In response to her nod in my direction he adds, "Oh yeah. Once we get over the bridge I might be safe saying that."

I cry, "Hey now. I'm still here. I don't think that was funny. Grams, I thought I was your favorite."

Mom walks in from the back porch and agrees, "I think Kirby has it from here. She is almost thirty-nine, after all."

If I kill both of them can I get away with it? If ABS didn't already know exactly how old I am, he does now.

Breaking the silence ABS asks, "Okay Kirby. Ready for an adventure to last a lifetime?"

"Sure. But according to her," shrugging my shoulder in Grams' direction, "that might not be long," I chide.

"Good point! We better get going."

The hour drive north to New Bern, North Carolina's first capital, through the rural town of Maysville, is fairly uneventful. Heading away from the beach, traffic moves smoothly as we drive a comfortable two miles per hour over the limit. Flat lands make way to rolling hills dotted with trees, isolated homes set back from the road, and country stores in varying stages of decay. Intersecting our drive in Pollocksville is the beautiful Trent river which makes a gentle turn as it moves from its origin in Kinston to join the Neuse River in New Bern. I remember this eastern part of the state as similar to other parts of the country I've visited. The deliberate river flowing through the back country reminds me of the lower Yellowstone River we rafted during one of our visits out west. Strange, but here, near sea level, we seem to have the same steady river as in the high country near the Wyoming Grand Tetons.

It's not as boring as driving through the California hills. At least there is life here. Besides that, I am riding with an incredibly handsome man.

When I ask if he always drives like an old woman, ABS puts it in perspective, "This old truck won't ever get me a ticket. I swear radar bounces off the banged up scraped bumper. Either that, or cops think I can't pay the fine, so they don't bother."

Tossing harmless barbs and jokes back and forth, I finally decide to tackle the elephant in the car. "So, young man, as I said before, I'm old enough to have been your babysitter and you were worried about taking me on a date until after we got over the bridge."

"Well, the age thing is in your mind, but the bridge, well that's another subject." After a pregnant pause he adds, "Just kidding I know the story of how you crashed your grandfather's beamer. But come on, who could blame you? I'm not sure what I would have done if I'd been lied to for fifteen years. Not to know who your birth dad was…, well, wow!"

"You know all that?"

"Sure Kirby. Grams and I are tight. And something else I'll tell you. I will never lie to you. Never. Okay?"

"Sounds great. So, since you know more about me than I thought, how about telling me about ABS. School, college, aspirations, children. Just threw that last one in to see if you were listening. Anything you want to tell me…."

Turning into the gas station to fill up, he ponders the request. It seems as if ABS is puzzling over how to respond as he cleans the windshield and finishes pumping. With the receipt in hand, he jumps in and begins, without prompting.

"High school was a non-starter. I hated most classes and thought the teachers were just collecting paychecks. So, I quit in the eleventh grade. My parents objected at first, but eventually relented and signed for me. They knew I would have stopped going anyway."

"Seriously?"

"Absolutely. I guess I thought I was smarter than my friends. I hadn't counted on a few things. First, there is still a lot of growing up to do, other than in classrooms. Then, I found out I couldn't play high school sports. Seems like they have a silly rule about attending classes to play. Bottom line: the principal was really upset and such a jerk! He forbade me from coming onto the school grounds. I guess he was upset I escaped his mini prison camp. Since I couldn't go to high school, I decided to try college."

"So, let me get this straight. You dropped out of high school and then went right to college?"

"I like to say, "transferred." I sort of skip the dropped-out piece. I took the placement tests at Craven Community College since I was living in New Bern. They weren't really equipped for me either. I started classes, but the counselors didn't know how to advise someone like me. Or maybe I wasn't really open to it. I talked with the dean but he seemed clueless to help. Sort of a trend back then with me. Anyway, I decided to do something else. But, you know what? We're getting close to Tryon Palace, so how about we skip the rest of the story and let me tell you about this place."

"Sounds good, but we have to go back to you later. I can't believe your parents let you quit. I especially want to hear about the kids and maybe even girlfriends." I wink adding, "Okay?"

"If you insist."

"I do."

Looking out the side window, I see numerous beautiful antebellum mansions. Driving the tree lined centuries old New Bern roads, ABS slows to a crawl at the corner of George and Pollock Street. I thought it was because of the stop sign, but as I shift my gaze from right to left, the palace majestically appears. This four story brick mansion, situated in the middle of a collection of other well-preserved nineteenth century homes, springs from beautifully manicured grounds behind a huge wall with tall iron gates. It's like being in England, or per-haps, what I remember of Colonial Williamsburg. I've also been to a twentieth century mansion in California called Hearst Castle. And, like many North Carolinians, I've visited The Biltmore Estate, one of the largest, most opulent private residences in the United States located in Asheville near the Blue Ridge Parkway. They each have their unique place. But this palace. Wow! I expect to see the changing of the guard any time although certainly not on the scale of Buckingham Palace. In fact, much, much smaller. The symmetrical palace building, with a circular drive, invites the image of horse drawn carriages. It is a bit more like Cinderella's home instead of the castle she danced in with Prince Charming. But this is a true North Carolina palace and it's been near my back yard since be-fore I was born. Like Charlestonians who never visit Fort Sumter, the South Carolina civil war national monument, it feels almost criminal not to have come here previously.

"Wow, this is beautiful. I can't wait to see the inside."

"Kirby, we will soon, but just know that Tryon Palace is much more than the building you saw as we drove by. So much more. We can spend all day just walking around the estate. There are other homes and buildings to visit, but today I think we'll stick with the main house and gardens. I don't want to overwhelm you."

Something was strange about how ABS said this, al-most as if he was taking me to his home. ABS parks his truck in the nearby lot where a costumed docent approaches us. I'm always guarded, even a bit uncomfortable, when I see people in costumes. Just a sign of the times, unfortunately. Although this person is wearing appropriate clothes for the location, I'm still a little freaked out as he comes near me, a bit closer than desired. From a distance of two feet, he gracefully extends his right arm, and with a gentle nod of his head asks, "Ma'am, Mr. Boucher, may I escort you to our palace?"

Feeling a bit uneasy but wanting to play along with the character, I agreeably offer my hand as we proceed to cross the cobblestone intersection leading to the mansion. Upon reaching the other side, the man carefully places my hand in the cradle of ABS' waiting arm, adding in chopped, crisp English, "I trust you will enjoy your moments in our modest manor."

ABS responds, "Thank you kindly Mr. Lindy. I'm sure we will."

I turned to look at ABS. When I glance back, our escort has disappeared, as if he had never been here.

Hands on my hips, I stammer, "Whoa! W...w... wait just a minute. What just happened? ABS, how in the world did he know your name? Better yet, how did you know his?"

Hiding a growing smirk, he sheepishly replies, "Oh that. I should have warned you. I've been here once or twice and some of the staff know me."

"Once or twice? From the sounds of it, you've been here a bunch. You have a little bit more to explain, mister."

"Okay, so I have been here a few times. In fact, my family home is just over there," pointing around the corner toward several beautifully maintained, multiple story clapboard sided homes.

"You've got to be kidding. Seriously. You couldn't think to mention this before? I thought you lived in a trailer at the Trav-L-Park."

Sensing my concern and knowing I don't like surprises, he calmly adds, "Just hear me out, please."

"I really *have* owned and lived in a trailer at Ronnie's for years. We've been friends since I was little. My dad bought the trailer when they were really cheap and I've kept it so I could have a place to crash for times when I tied one on at the E Club. That's one reason I didn't mind helping your Grams. It was just up the beach, literally. The lot we parked in today used to be owned by my grandfather, until he deeded it to the foundation. Grandpa was the chief architect of the 1950s Tryon Palace reconstruction. Remember me telling you he was a master craftsman – all true. Come on, we have a private showing planned just for you."

I wonder what comes next as we continue walking. The promenade is gorgeous as it blends into the circular drive. I imagine elegantly dressed eighteenth and nineteenth century aristocrats and upper class New Bernians enjoying the beauty of this oasis in an otherwise untamed territory filled with wild animals. Hesitantly walking up the pea gravel driveway, I envision carriages pulled by handsome geldings while ladies with high-waisted, multi-layered dresses are escorted up the nine large cement steps onto the covered portico to be met there by a smartly dressed man servant.

I hear ABS asking, "Are you okay Kirby?" and realize I'm almost in a trance. This is so cool having all the people dressed up in period appropriate attire. I guess I'll have to get over the fact that my tour guide for the day is wearing blue jeans and a polo. At least he's *my* tour guide! Okay, so my imagination may be running a little wild too. But it really is quite exciting.

"Oh, sorry ABS. I'm okay, just lost in my thoughts. I didn't know how impressive the palace is and we haven't even stepped inside. Why don't more people come here?"

"Great question Kirby. I wonder too, especially about people who live in the area. It seems that those who have lived here for a long time and their families don't think of this as a real palace. They actually wonder, w*hy would I want to visit a fake palace?* I've spent many hours nursing a beer with locals explaining how important it is to keep our eastern North Carolina heritage and ancestors' stories alive. One response I often hear is that Tryon isn't really a palace. Locals, with deep ancestral roots, say it is really just a big house and is called a palace out of spite. They believe the then governor taxed the residents to pay for his overindulgence when he built the estate.

"How interesting," I say adding, "So even back then we had..., what's the word for it?"

"Pork Barrel politics?"

"Exactly," I reply. "So, the governor used Colonists' money to build it."

"I guess that's a good way to look at it. But come on. It was built in the late eighteenth century. I wish people would get over it. Anyway, we'll enjoy it, even if they won't."

Just then, a middle-aged, colonial costumed, servant opens the twelve-foot-tall wooden door to greet us. "Good afternoon Mr. Boucher. It is so good to have you back. And whom is this lovely young lady accompanying you?"

At least the gentleman got it right when he said, "YOUNG" lady. He could have ruined the entire afternoon asking, "Is this your older sister?" or worse, "Is this your mother?"

"Good afternoon Jason," ABS replied. "This is my good friend, Kirby, from Emerald Isle. We'll be touring the palace today and spending time in the gardens."

"Very good, sir. Shall we bring your boat to the dock? And will you be visiting your family home today? Mister McClease asked whether you will be dining with us - perhaps some banana pudding tonight?"

Laughing, ABS replies, "Not today. Please tell him I look forward to tasting his pudding in due time. We might visit another building, if time allows. We intend to head back to the island in the late afternoon."

With a nod of his head he replies, "Yes sir. We'll be here if you need anything. G'day Mr. Boucher, Ms. Fontaine."

As ABS turns to walk through the open door, I grab his arm a bit more forcefully than intended and say a bit louder than expected, "Hold it right there, mister. Before I step one foot in this place, you have some more explaining to do. First, who are you really? Second, bring boat to the dock? Third, family house? And thirdly. Wait a minute. Fourth. You never told him my last name. So how is it he called me Ms. Fontaine? I'm little more than creeped out right now and think perhaps I should go. You know, they make movies about weird stuff like this." As an afterthought I add, "And now that I think about it, someone's been watching me for the past few months. Anyone I might be standing near?"

With his usual calm demeanor which was infuriating me even more ABS replied, "Kirby, relax. Please. I can explain. But first, what's this about someone watching you?"

"Not now. Don't try to change the subject. Explain the boat and all the other stuff first!"

"I didn't want to confuse you given what you're going through. Obviously you have a lot on your mind. Frankly, I've had several women interested in me simply because of what I have and not who I am. It's refreshing to get to know someone interested in me!"

"Good start! Boat? House? Name? Take your pick."

"Okay. I have some money left to me from my grandfather. Much of it is in a trust. He made a ton leading restoration projects up and down the east coast and invested wisely. He even consulted on the Biltmore Estate and other private property renovations across the country. Most of his money went to the Palace Foundation where he served on the board of directors. He loved New Bern and hoped to ensure everyone will see the charm and beauty of our state's first capital. He loved Tryon Palace the most! *My* family house, which is really the four story building behind you, is called The Dixon House."

"Oh My God. Seriously? The home on the corner of the palace grounds is your family's?"

"It was! It appears I'm the last direct descendant of my great, great, great Uncle George Dixon on my mother's side. George was a rich New Bern businessman until the early 1830s when he lost everything. He even once had to foreclose on the home but was able to buy it back later. See the widow's walk between the two chimneys? It's said on some nights you can see something or someone standing at the far end gazing forlornly toward the Trent River."

"That's scary and a bit sad."

"Well it was almost two hundred years ago. I've only seen her once or twice, and not in a long time. I was scared the first time, but there are so many other freaky mysteries in New Bern I just accept it."

Grabbing his arm a little tighter I ask, "Seriously?"

"Seriously. But we'll get to those later. So much for the history lesson. The house was ours, but it is now deeded to the foundation. When I die, and I plan that to happen late in the next century, the foundation owns it outright. Yes, we maintain a small boat the board can use, primarily to attract donors and other supporters. But seriously, I think you know by now I don't flaunt money and detest those who do. Finally, I want to ensure you have a wonderful time so I made certain the first person-character interpreters knew your name and addressed you properly. The rest of the tour, unfortunately, is up to me."

"Good start. How small a boat?"

"I think it is fifty-six feet."

"Did you say fifty-six feet?"

"Yes Kirby. But remember, others use it too."

"Whatever... You could let the President of the United States use that big a boat." I'm not sure what to think or do. I'm used to being around people of means, but not people who can go to a palace and command a yacht, whenever they want. "Okay mister. No more surprises or I leave. Deal?"

"Deal!"

"One more thing, what about the banana pudding?"

"I almost forgot," he said, throwing his head back and laughing out loud. "Keith McClease, who has served as the palace's master gardener and caretaker for nearly forty years, also makes the best banana pudding in New Bern. The problem is, at least three times in the past few years when he has made banana pudding someone who ate it died shortly afterwards. I don't mean that day or even that week. But within close proximity to eating the pudding, someone died. Coincidence or not, every time he offers I say I would love to in due time – like thirty years. We've been joking about it for years. And nope, no banana pudding today!"

"With my luck ABS, I totally agree. This is not the time to try banana pudding." No telling if Karma might suddenly reappear. Don't want to tempt her for sure.

With a smile, the first in the past few minutes, I cautiously offer my hand as we ascend nine steps into the eighteenth century.

"Absolutely splendid. Beautiful. Oh My God. How did they do this? Where did they find these? Are they authentic?" Comments pour out as we begin our tour. I'm captivated by the ornate portraits rivaling museum quality. Entering the ballroom, ABS points out the King and Queen of England staring at us from ten-foot tall portraits. "Carlotta Regina" is inscribed above the picture.

Pointing to her, he whispers, "Queen Charlotte. Our Queen City, Charlotte, is named for her."

"Cool" I whisper, still in awe.

"Speaking of cool, let me show you our original air conditioning," he replied.

"No way. They didn't have air conditioning. I don't think Ben Franklin had even flown his kite yet."

"Funny! Actually he had, although no one had figured out how to harness electricity. Look over here."

Pulling out huge wooden hurricane type shutters from inside the walls, similar to old fashioned pocket doors, ABS slid them on tracks beside near floor length glass windows. "In the hot summer afternoons, servants pull these out and slide them across the windows preventing the sun from heating the rooms. They used fireplaces in most rooms for that. The shutters also keep out the cold which tried to slip in through the single pane glass. What's fascinating is that Pops, and other preservationists, made these shutters exactly like those used two hundred years ago with old fashioned tools – no electricity. The two-foot thick wall also helps preserve the antiques and other artifacts. This is what we refer to as original North Carolina climate control."

From the front doorway, my guide escorts me to the elaborate main staircase which is ornately decorated and handsomely constructed, without using a single nail.

"Wow ABS, this reminds me of Hogwarts."

"Only you would think that, Kirby. Although I really have heard a few children mention Harry Potter when they came in here."

True to himself, ABS takes me up the "Lesser Steps" which servants and "lesser" people use. These are narrow and much steeper. People using them would likely be carrying large loads such as food from the kitchen, or even furniture. Hanging on these walls, out of the way, but available if needed, are leather bound fire baskets, usually filled with sand or water in mansions such as this.

"Kirby, see the baskets hanging on the wall? One of our mysteries is why none were found in the rubble when Tryon Palace burned in 1798. Some people think they may have been pilfered by squatters, while others suggest a more sinister conspiracy. British sympathizers may have targeted New Bern in revenge for losing the colonies."

Lost in the history and hanging on every word ABS shares, I stroll leisurely from room to room imagining living here two hundred years ago. It's remarkable how they've reconstructed everything and created a "living museum".

ABS explains how the palace is patterned after a fine European mansion although it is not nearly as large as some might imagine. Originally built for the Royal Governor, William Tryon, by English architect John Hawks, the governor desired a home similar to the fine London homes he was accustomed to. Unfortunately, he was reassigned as Governor of New York and enjoyed the palace for only a year. Governor Martin replaced him and lived in the mansion for several years but left hurriedly at the beginning of the Revolutionary War.

As period dressed characters move quietly about the palace and grounds, ABS explains how, and why, the foundation rebuilt it from the ground floor nearly one hundred and fifty years after it burned.

"It burned all the way to the ground. Luckily the previous governor kept meticulous records of everything in the house and took them when he left prior to the fire. New Bern town fathers also held several auctions of the remaining assets to help pay maintenance expenses. Auction documents have been helpful in locating original articles, too. The Foundation used these records to collect authentic replacements during the reconstruction. You know, we have artifacts from President Washington's visit to New Bern in 1791."

"ABS, I heard once if George Washington stayed in all the places claiming he visited he would have been nearly two hundred years old when he died.

"Funny. But he *did* stay here."

Continuing, ABS adds, "After George's visit and the fire in 1798, the ensuing years were difficult. The grounds and buildings were used for a variety of occupations including a stable, accounting firm, and more."

As we move from room to room, I'm more and more fascinated with the history and elegance of this palace.

"ABS, where did they get all the pictures. Everything looks like they should be in museums."

"Well, if you think about it, they sort of are."

"Good point. Just look at the period clocks, books, china, silver, antique furniture, and pianos and other musical instruments in the parlor. They all look authentic and must have taken a lot of work to acquire."

"They really aren't even finished. Thanks to the relentless pursuit of New Bern native, Mrs. James Latham, and her establishment of the Palace restoration fund, the state supports our ongoing restoration project. Years ago, the twenty-five member Tryon Palace Commission earnestly took on Mrs. Latham's vision. First they located the original plans by tracking down the architect's descendants. Surveyors and construction engineers located the original foundation cornerstone so they could start reconstruction on the exact spot. At the same time, historians and museum curators began scouring the world for actual artifacts or replicas. One other fun fact is the reconstruction effort required relocation of fifty buildings, including businesses and squatters. Can you believe they even got permission to relocate the highway that ran through the grounds? That would be nearly impossible today. See the bridge through the window? It goes to James City now, but it used to cross right over there," pointing to a section of water extending past the beautiful back lawn.

"That's amazing, especially knowing that a woman was leading this movement."

"Exactly! Women were barely able to vote when Mrs. Lathram initiated her plan. I never met her of course, but my grandfather spoke of her with great admiration. He said she died just before the project was finished."

After a pause, as if trying to figure out exactly what to say, ABS adds, "To put it in perspective Kirby, we got to the moon faster than we finished rebuilding Tryon Palace. And we aren't really finished. We continuously work on other buildings and the estate gardens."

"So, other than your family owning the Dixon Place, how did your family get involved in the Foundation?"

"Remember my telling you about my grandfather?"

"Uh huh.""

"Well, Pops was one of the first craftsman to work on the site. Other than getting approval, the longest part of the work was the restoration of the main building, which he oversaw. Now, it looks like a magnificent two hundred and fifty-year old mansion. Really, it's only about seventy years old."

"They've done a great job making it look and feel much older."

Entranced, I'm beginning to forget the creepy feeling I felt a few hours ago. As we walk through the rooms, I see wall deterioration which I thought was representative of the original building. ABS explains that some of the exterior walls have new leaks, but the Foundation has more difficulty than average home owners getting them repaired.

"The Foundation is trying to find an experienced craftsman and historically accurate building material to repair it in the same manner that they rebuilt it. We have to repair it to what the U. S. Department of the Interior refers to as "like with like". These guidelines ensure the building and gardens are as nearly authentic as the artifacts we place in it. In addition to the splendid woodworking on the stairs and walls, period air conditioning using specially made windows and doors, and our beautiful views of the river, the collection of period replacements or replicas of the art work, furniture, libraries, and china is tremendous. We constantly and relentlessly search for pieces used in the pre-fire inventory."

Several hours later, I'm still fascinated but mentally exhausted. "Amazing. How about some fresh air?"

"Absolutely," he replies with a wink and smile.

I return the wink, feeling much more comfortable. Maybe it's being out of a big old mansion with scary staircases and people walking around in costumes. Or, maybe having been creeped out for the last two months, thinking someone was watching me…. Well, being outside just seems a little safer.

The kitchen, blacksmith shop, and even the old chicken coop, since converted into a gift shop, are interesting. Having toured all of these, I have a deeper appreciation for people who lived then. I couldn't have survived. Wandering through the gardens we walk along the grounds' outer edge, near the river.

ABS continues, "If you can imagine, in colonial times our back property extended well into the river to allow for off-loading of ships. Our property still extends into the river. We allow the city to maintain the road along the river behind us for traffic control."

"I've never seen such beautiful gardens. I've seen Hearst, Williamsburg, and even The Biltmore. Sure, they're huge but these are perfect! Pappy would be so envious."

"I'm glad you like them. I'll ensure Keith tells his crew. Want to hear more about them?"

"Sure."

"Well, I'm not the best person to tell you, but I'll do my best. I know we have several types of gardens. To our left we have the traditional formal garden of the England eighteenth century. We also have a spring garden that offers more traditional daffodils, tulips and spring flowers. My favorite is the colonial era garden with colorful displays of marigolds, celosia, and seasonal vegetables, which are used in the kitchen."

"I didn't know you were so fond of the flowers. Perhaps I'm seeing a different side of you."

"I'm told anything goes these days," he jokes. "Seriously, this is not my strongest point and I can get more details if you want."

"Kirby, this is the coolest thing in the garden. Check out this living fence. See how the apple tree branches are hand twisted into fences for other plants to grow on? This kind of fencing is still used in third world countries like Nicaragua and is time appropriate for the palace."

"Too cool. But do you think all of these gardens were really here? Seems like a lot of work without having the tools we have now."

"Two answers to your question. Truthfully, the original plans don't show this many gardens. It seems the early restoration team wanted more gardens than was thought to have been here. The designer had worked on the Mount Vernon gardens and wanted a more colonial style influence. I know my grandfather was not in favor of including anything not authentic since he was being held to a near perfect restoration standard for the palace building. Secondly, back then, they might have had indentured servants, and even slaves during part of the time, to care for the gardens. So, I'm not sure the size and scope was that big of a deal."

"Who wouldn't love these gardens? But, it sure is hot. I'm not sure I would have made it as a lady in this court-yard and definitely not a peasant or stable girl."

I love the history and charm of the building, the archaic functional kitchen, and, of course, the colorful gardens... and visiting the blacksmith hut on the edge of the property is pretty neat too. ABS suggests they built it away from other wooden buildings that might accidentally be set on fire. *Good idea*, I thought, now knowing the Tryon Palace history.

Inside his hut, a sweaty, dirty blacksmith hunches over the flame using ancient bellows to fan his fire. With the hot iron, he forms historically appropriate tools, knobs, buttons, and other replicas for the estate and other histori-cal locations.

ABS senses my intrigue. "They sell some of their hardware and make other items for places throughout the region that don't have their own blacksmith shop. New Bern has many historic sites that require period pieces and this shop pays for itself, which is a good thing since it costs a lot of money to run the estate."

My favorite place on the palace grounds is the stable. Used for a variety of businesses over the centuries, the original red brick walls with massive curved stable doors are impressive. They remind me of the reconstructed sta-bles used in downtown Charleston for horse and buggy tours. I imagine Clydesdales marching out with their dal-matian close behind. But these - these are hundreds of years old historic walls and doors. It's fascinating!

"You ready to see something else?"

"Sure, whatcha got in mind?"

"So, I told you the palace is really this building, but the estate has more homes. I thought we could look at another one. One that is really haunted."

"**Not** a good idea with what I've been through."

"Good point, so I'll tell you later about the mulatto servant child that was kept in the attic."

"Stop, I don't want to hear it."

Smiling he says, "Just kidding. He didn't live there."

After another pause he adds, "He died there."

I smack him on the arm and think I hurt myself more than I did him.

"Okay. I'm kidding, but at least let me tell you about it or another palace haunting while we enjoy a drink in the kitchen of the Dissoway building."

"Okay. So, why is it called 'Dissoway?'"

"Well, years ago when people would ask where it is they would respond, "Dissoway." Actually it's the name of one of the well-to-do families who owned the home we're standing in."

"That's one really bad joke."

As we drank our Pepsi, ABS began to share another of his supernatural stories.

"One of the stories I like the most is about Emeline, a female Confederate spy who haunts The Jones House. During the Civil War, the house was used as a Yankee prison for southern prisoners. Not many people know this, but New Bern fell to the Union Forces so early it was occupied and therefore saved from General Sherman's destruction, unlike many of its southern sister cities."

"So it's a good thing to lose early, if you're going to lose, I guess."

"That's one morbid way to think about it. Anyway, I'll continue, if there are no more anticipated interruptions. Well, Emeline really didn't die in the prison. She actually died of old age, right down the road in Carteret County. But it's said she haunts the house because of what supposedly happened to her while held by the Yankees!"

"What does she do?"

"Something so sinister and scary only one person alive has ever experienced it and is alive to tell."

"Go ahead," I say, a bit on edge.

"Well. It seems that when a certain person, who comes from an old New Bern family thought to have been involved with the prison, is in the building, Emeline purposefully opens the cross-shaped hot water faucet until the water flows. She causes a metal on metal grinding sound with no mistaking what it is. If the individual reacts too quickly and turns it off, Emeline turns it back on until she's finished. It doesn't seem to happen to anyone else."

"That's not that spooky."

"Want to go back?" he asks.

"Nope. I guess it's spooky enough that I don't need to see it. But forget all this talk about ghosts. It's close to dinner time and I'm getting hungry. What's a girl have to do to get something to eat?"

"I thought you'd never ask. I'm a little wary of offering anything else in case you bolt and leave me alone."

"I'm long past that, if there are no more surprises, today! Plus, you drove."

"There is that," he replies with a smirk.

"Well, it's almost five o'clock. I've loved everything today, but our little snack we had on the way up is just about gone."

"Say no more. Adios New Bern. We'll walk around the town and rest of our buildings another day. I'd love to take you to the birthplace of Pepsi, our North Carolina History Center, and eat at Baker's Kitchen. One of my good friends owns it. I promise we'll get the best and biggest breakfast this side of your Grams' house. They have one breakfast called the *Hungry Farmer* that will fill you up."

Walking across the courtyard, the stares of several envious female guests and even a few palace employees burn into my backside as they watch our every move. Maybe not both of our moves. I can enjoy this for now and decide to show them that even *older ladies* can hold their own. Interlacing my left hand fingers in his right, I reach over and massage his forearm as we stroll through the gate into the twenty-first century.

Yep, all mine. Choke on this ladies, I think. Jealousy is not becoming, but it certainly is better on the other foot.

The afternoon sun is falling, bringing the temperature down to about eighty degrees. I had not realized how hot it was as we walked through the gardens. Once ABS gets the truck air conditioning blasting, I feel refreshed. As we pass the North Carolina History Center and head toward Highway 70 south, ABS looks out the window and says, "Yep. We'll come back here and spend an entire day in there. For now, I have a surprise in store for you."

Dropping his hand, which I had taken as we started down the road, I blurt, "Huh? Didn't we talk about no more..."

Interrupting quickly ABS said, "Poor word choice; sorry! I have a *treat* in store."

"Better!" I smile and add, "So what's the treat?"

"Ever hear of El's Diner in Morehead City?"

"Nope, but I believe I'm getting ready for a surprise."

"Treat, not a surprise," he corrects me quickly.

"Humph. Good catch. Mind if I lay my head on your shoulder for a little while? I'm beat."

"My pleasure."

"Oh, and by the way, how about turtle watching with Journey. Is it okay for him to go with you?"

"Sure. I'll come by your place on the way and pick him up about six next Saturday morning. We'll probably get some breakfast before we go fishing or skim boarding. Okay?"

"Okay by me. He adores you. It hasn't been easy on him with Sam passing. Moving back here without his friends has been rough too. But he's such a great kid. Sure, he has Mom, Dad, and Grams, but, well, you know this is tough for all of us."

"I get it Kirby. I really do. I adore him too."

"Thanks! Wake me up when we get close so I can freshen up."

"Ha," he laughs although I have no idea why. He could have said he adored *me* too…

Chapter 18

El's Diner

"Wake up sleepy head. We're here."

"Noooo; I said wake me so I could freshen up. You promised."

Looking around quickly, I think I know why he laughed earlier.

Parked in a dark gravel lot on the bend of a busy highway in Morehead City, there must be fifty other cars beside, ahead, behind, and practically on top of us. This must be what going to an old-fashioned drive-in theater was like. Getting my bearings, I notice we're across the street from Carteret Community College where several of my high school friends studied Marine Biology. In the rearview mirror, I see a backwards reflection of the Carteret County hospital and under the trees to my right there is a couple making out. I vaguely remember those days. To our right, under the sprawling gnarled oak trees whose limbs nearly touch the ground before rising back toward the sky, the shrouded street light casts shadows on a family of kids playing, while their parents wait on their order.

"You're going to love this Kirby. I've been coming here for years. It's the best barbecue this side of Lexington."

Just then, a curvaceous, two-toned blonde, lipstick wearing, Jezebel of a carhop, strolls to his car window. In her skimpy waitress outfit, and despite running from car to car all day, this girl is still smokin' hot and way too flirtatious.

Leaning against the window's edge and smacking her bubblegum, she smiles and asks, "Hi Hon, where you been keeping yourself? Having the usual or are you trying something different tonight?"

She didn't even glance my way. Good thing. I'm not sure what I might have said.

I heard the "having the usual" in her snarky voice and telepathically sent every mean thought I could muster, while smiling right through her. Mom taught me well.

Leaning out the window, a bit too close for my liking, ABS orders, "Two huge barbecue sandwiches, one with slaw and one without. You know how I like it! Two orders of hush puppies and cherry cokes. Thanks sweetheart."

Coldly I ask, "Huh? You know how I like it? *Sweetheart*?"

"Sorry Kirby. You caught me. I confess..." Smiling he adds, "Vicki's my cousin on my mom's side. You'll like her when you get to know her. She's been really protective of me, ever since. Well. Never mind."

"What? Ever since what?"

"Another time. Okay? Give me this and I promise no more surprises."

"Okay. This one." I'm not happy about it. There's something still nagging in the back of my head. Someone's been watching me and ABS either conveniently forgot to answer or knew more than he was saying when I mentioned it.

Like a bickering couple married for forty years, we sit in silence for what seems to be hours. I know sometimes it's just better to not say anything, especially since I was already wrong about his cousin.

Vicki delivers the food in brown paper bags and we devour it. ABS is right. This barbecue is some of the best I've ever tasted. Things finally get back to normal by the time we finish eating, whatever normal is.

Breaking the silence, ABS turns on the radio and asks, "Did you enjoy your sandwich?"

"Seriously ABS, that was some of the best food I've ever eaten. It was as good as Grams, which I can't believe I'm saying. I'm amazed we never came to El's when we visited Pappy's Place during the summers. It reminds me of what Pappy would have said, "Go to the hole in the wall for the best food in town." I add, "Twice today you've shown me places I should have known about. I can't believe I've never been to them."

"Stick around. Perhaps I'll show you more... So, you really like it? I'm glad! El's been in the same spot more than fifty years. There are other really good drive-ins around the Crystal Coast, but none pile barbecue or shrimp burgers as high. Service is awesome too. Of course having Vicki here doesn't hurt. Guys like her, and I get great service."

"About that. I'm really sorry. I thought she was flirting. And I worried she might think I was your mom."

"Too funny. That means you would be her aunt. By the way, read the note she slipped in the bag."

Feeling even more like an idiot, I read aloud, "Hey Cuz. Is this the girl everybody's talking about? They're right. She's really pretty! Even with her shirt on. Good luck. Don't do anything I wouldn't... Luv ya, Vic."

I can't feel any smaller than I do now. How do I get out of this? I feel like a teenager. I decide to attack it head on and totally avoid it.

"ABS, I loved the food and the company was even better. I think by now you may have noticed that I don't need impressing. I sort of like things simple, always have."

"Me too, Kirby. And I think it's cute that you were a little bit jealous."

Hoping it will just float away, I continue to ignore his previous comment and reply, "I had a wonderful day. But how in the heck am I going to work off all this food? Thanks so much for taking me to Tryon Palace. I can't wait to go back with Journey. By then I can work of some pounds and afford to try the bakery."

Laughingly ABS replies, "You look great and it's actually called Baker's Kitchen. They have great desserts, but it's a full service restaurant. You'll love it. We'll definitely take Journey. I had a great time, too."

Without realizing what I'm doing, I reach across the truck's center console and take ABS' right hand, which had been resting on his leg. Maybe he was thinking the same thing.

"You okay?" I ask.

"Better than I've been in a while. I really like you, Kirby. I have since I met you at the airport. Today was great! Maybe we can do it again soon?"

Reaching up, I answer him with a tender kiss on the cheek. I haven't forgotten we had arrived and are parked in Grams' driveway. And, I haven't forgotten my husband died only six months ago. I'm trying to practice what Grams has been reminding me for the past few days, "You need to get back in the saddle and move on."

I thoroughly enjoyed myself and want to let this moment linger. It feels strange, yet exhilarating, to be close to a man again. Stroking his bangs back across his forehead, I feel ABS tense just a bit as I touch his cheek and slide my hand along his tanned and muscular shoulders.

"ABS, you are a very special person. Yes, we can do it again soon. I really like you, too."

Gently holding my face with his powerful hands, he reaches over and kisses me deeply, until I gasp for breath.

On cue, the porch light comes on. We giggle like high school freshmen, wondering who might be inside watching.

Standing in palm tree shadows, as if hiding from my parents, ABS gently pulls me into a deeper embrace and kisses me passionately. I feel my body reacting, as it has not for a while. I'm sure ABS needs to leave, quickly. As he turns to go back to his truck, my hand lingers on his arm. I say with a sense of urgency, "You need to go." He senses why and continues to move away. I watch him with much stronger feelings than anticipated. I return his wave and feel like a co-ed dating the football captain. I'm sure my face shows it too. Turning to our front door, I see Journey waiting on the porch.

Journey was happier for me than I expected. He had seen everything and, while missing his dad, knows we both need to move on. Grams, Mom, and Dad all spent time with him recently and I think my going on this date was exactly what we both needed. We stayed up late talking about how much we both miss Sam. Journey put it in perspective.

"Dad's never coming home. He wouldn't want you to be a miserable young woman. If the roles were reversed, he would be sad and moping for a while. I've been moping recently, but a few days ago I thought about one of those silver lining quotes he used to tell me when I was hacking around the golf course. To help get me back on my game he would say, "The sun won't shine until you put the umbrella away... Be free." It always made me realize I need to stop worrying about what already happened and look toward my next shot. Dad wants you to be free to start taking another shot. Mom, you should feel fine about dating ABS."

Is that what I'm doing, dating? I guess I am. It hadn't really occurred to me that others might think I am. I thought I was just going out with a friend. Tonight changed that, I guess.

As we spoke, the phone rang.

"Take it Mom. I'll be right back. I'm going to grab a snack."

"Hey ABS. Yes, I had a great time too. Yes, Journey met me at the door. We've been talking since you left."

"Wow, that's a long time. I hope everything's okay."

"Yep, it is a long time, but so needed. No, it's fine. He is actually very happy for me... for us."

"Us?"

"Well, I meant Journey and me. But, yes. I'm sure he means you as well. He loves having you around. I look forward to seeing you again, soon. Thanks for calling. Journey's coming back now. Thanks again. Sleep well."

Chapter 19

Caribsea

Phew, after several weeks of waiting, the sellers and bank finally accepted my offer for an all cash short sale allowing us to close quickly. While the current owners are losing, we are getting a great deal. An ocean front, two story beach cottage with four bedrooms, an office, a Jacuzzi and an elevator. The only thing missing is a garage. I think I have an inside track with a carpenter who may be able to figure out a way to enclose the carport so we can store our extra furniture, Journey's scooter, and my car. We'll close in early September, which, after the tourists are gone will be a great time for a celebration cookout on the beach.

Journey's excited because there are several turtle nests nearby, which means they may come back next year and he can watch them daily. Speaking of Journey, today is the big day. ABS picked him up early this morning to go on his turtle patrol. He looked so cute wearing his turtle patrol shirt – ABS, not Journey. Next year maybe Journey will get one.

With both of them gone for the day, I'm headed for fun in the sun. Car purchased, house waiting to close, son figuring it out, and ABS... Well let's just say we are in the right place at the right time.

"Hey Mom, you going to the beach?" I yell as she walks down the hall carrying a load of clothes.

"Not today Kirby. This is my catch-up day. With everything that happened during the past few weeks, I'm way behind. Go ahead and enjoy yourself."

"Okay then. Bye"

I also check in on Grams before heading out. Relaxing in her newly fashioned waiting area, she is busy writing the novel she began recently. Grams fancies herself the next Grandma Moses of writing. Maybe she will be. She has quite a sense of humor and has definitely lived a full and eventful life. A year with Pappy might have felt like seven years with another man. Or maybe that's the dog year's equivalency. We always joked about how busy he was, before he died. Regardless, Grams has lots of material from which to choose. A few weeks ago, she told us how she learned artists painting scenes of the Emerald Isle bridge are called "plein air" or, *outside in full air*, artists. She jokingly decided she would be a *plein air* writer and began typing her story as she sat on the front porch. I'm not sure that's the correct French translation. Like Pappy, Grams enjoys telling her joke to everyone she sees.

"See you later Grams. I'm headed down to the beach. Need anything?"

"No baby girl. You enjoy yourself. I'm not at a good stopping point. Make sure you wear plenty of sunscreen."

Flippantly, I holler going downstairs, "You bet. You already told ABS I'm old. No reason to wrinkle early, too. Love you Grams."

With beach chair, snacks, magazines, umbrella, and, of course, sunscreen loaded in the beach cart, I head down our path through the sand dunes. Unexpectedly, my phone rings. Once again, no one is on the other end. Oh well, wrong number. This is the fifth or sixth time in the past week and is getting tiresome!

I set up my beach camp hoping Journey and ABS will join me later. It sure is easier when there are other people to help. I manage to screw the umbrella deep into the sand and anchor it by pulling the cart beside it. I hate to think of impaling other sunbathers if a gust of wind lifts my umbrella airborne. It happens every year, somewhere, and frightens me to think I might cause it.

Brother it is hot! Then again, I am at the beach in the middle of summer. Salty sweat pushes sunscreen into my eyes, causing them to burn and tear. Dabbing both with a damp towel only makes it worse, so I rinse them by pouring my bottled water into one, then the other. They feel a little better and by facing directly into the wind I get them to stop stinging. Roasting under the sun, I toss and turn, purposefully trying to even out my tan. Occasionally, I jump into the umbrella shade, then quickly race to the water, without burning my feet on the sweltering sand. Then

I repeat the process. It's like being a pig on a spit or getting s'mores marshmallows just right. Over and over and over until the appropriate shade of brown, without catching fire. This is what tanning is all about – what fun!

I wonder to myself, *why do we do this?*

As the tide changes and waves encroach on my stakeout, I realize I've been in the sun nearly five hours. That's way too long! That means Journey's been gone for over seven hours without a call. I hope they're okay. Oh no. I realize I'm becoming more like Grams and Mom when I wonder if they put on sunscreen. As soon as that thought crosses my mind, I hear Journey yelling at me from the dunes guarding Pappy's Place.

"Hey Mom. You coming up soon?"

"Hi Baby." Whoops. "Hi Journey." He's reminded me several times this summer he's too old to be "Baby." At least on the beach. "Come on down and tell me about your day."

"Be there in a few…" Journey brought his beach chair and sat down under the umbrella which told me he knew he'd been in the sun too long. He excitedly began sharing his experience.

"Mom, it was super fantastic," a term he had learned from his father, which he had not used for months. "We started walking the beach a little after six o'clock. Within a few minutes we spotted a fresh crawl. I'd never seen one before and it was awesome. ABS had seen plenty so he knew right away it was a dry crawl, meaning the mother turtle looked for a spot but didn't lay her eggs. He called it in anyway. When the team that verifies the nests arrived we continued our walk. Halfway to Randy's Way we spotted another crawl. This one was more promising. It had an entry point in the sand that looks like a single motorcycle tread. The track pushed across the sand to an area where it appears she may have laid her eggs before making a turn and heading back toward the ocean. The survey team checked it out, too and we were right. We'll be able to watch for the next fifty days until they hatch. So, I won't have to wait until next year."

"Wow. Sounds exciting. What else did you do?"

"Well, we still had to finish the walk. And, we found a third crawl. ABS was excited too. He told me I could walk with him anytime. Seems like I might be a good luck charm he said. When ABS asked on the beach if anyone wanted to look at the turtle tracks, plenty of people did, especially girls."

I'm sure they did, thinking to myself. *Calm down old woman. He was with your son!*

"Well, after the turtle walk we went skim boarding. The tide was high and there were no waves, so it was perfect to ride at the water's edge. Then we drove out to Fort Macon. ABS knows everyone there, including the superintendent. He introduced me to Ranger Lewis who said I could help out the rest of the summer. I just have to find a way to get there because it is too far on my scooter. ABS said we'd figure it out."

"What will they let you do?"

"There are a couple of things they asked me to think about. I can set up an education booth near the beach access and tell everyone about the kinds of turtles we have, how they nest, and other stuff. They have three nests already which should hatch in the middle of September. The ranger said I'm really too young to be on the patrol, but I can help when I come to the fort by checking to make sure people don't mess with the nests. I hope to go once or twice a week. And, he said I can participate in the Civil War reenactments they put on several times a year. There's one coming up soon. I can be a drummer or possibly even carry a rifle. He has to check on that."

"Wow, you sure do have some big plans. Are you okay with all of this responsibility? How about meeting new friends here and hanging around the house until our place is ready?"

"It's only once or twice a week. Say it's okay Mom. I told him you would agree."

"Of course it's fine with me, but we need to figure out the transportation plans. This sounds like very responsible positions and you can't let them down. What else did you do?"

"Well, after we rode ABS' Fat Boy to the fort, he took me to the Coast Guard station. Seems like he knows lots of the guys there, too. A couple even said, "Hi Seal" instead of ABS, which sounded weird."

"I know about that and have been meaning to ask him. What's a Fat Boy?"

"Oh, that's his Harley. He said I can ride with him once or twice, but real men don't ride with real men, or something like that."

"Hmmm. I'll ask about that too."

"Well, I got to see the Coast Guard drug interdiction boats, rescue equipment, jet skis, barracks, and all sorts of neat things. It was like being back at Dad's squadron. Mom, I never realized the Coasties, that's what ABS calls them, are like Marines with all sorts of jobs and missions. The Chief Petty Officer said I could stop by anytime I'm out at the fort, as long as I have my military ID."

"That sounds really cool. Seems like you packed ten gallons into a five-gallon hat," one of Pappy's old expressions.

"We did. It was so much fun."

"How about lunch. Did you eat?"

"Saved the best for last Mom. You know Caribsea, the new restaurant across from Highway 58 Bikes, on the way to the pier?"

"The one that looks like a ship?"

"That's it. You'll never guess where we went for lunch."

Kidding I ask, "I have no idea, where?"

"Ha ha; just for that I'm not telling you. Okay, since you pressured me. ABS took me there and you'll never guess what I learned."

Smarter than a minute ago, I say, "You're right young man. What did you learn?"

"Mom, while we ate on the third deck, which means floor in sailor talk, ABS told me all about the building, how it was named, and even more about the ship it was named after. Have you heard the story?"

"No Sweetie I haven't. It wasn't finished until after we got back and I haven't had a chance to go." Maybe ABS can take me soon, I thought.

"That's funny," he said, although I'm not sure what was funny.

"Well, ABS can tell it better than me, but this is what I remember."

"First he showed me how the inside railings of the building look like the outside railings of a ship. It's upscale and very modern, with NASCAR pictures, plaques, and other cool things. The furniture in the waiting area and the office with smoked glass remind me of Gram's kidney doctor's office. Then we took the elevator up to the main dining room. There's a huge port hole with a brass telescope you can look through in the lobby. It looks right out at the Emerald Isle bridge. ABS told me they considered "The Bridge" as one of the names for the restaurant, although it was in reference to the part of a ship. Oh yeah, I forgot. The entire building is owned by this cool company that does something with helping people get better deals when they ship stuff. It's called Transportation Impact. I think they're like FedEx, only better."

"Wow, so the whole building is built like a ship?"

"That's what it's supposed to be. The top floor is an outside eating area you would like. You can look over the homes into the Sound and see the ocean from the other side. ABS said they are known for being a restaurant that is, "not just fine dining." This restaurant is the chef's dream. In fact, the chef came out and said something about his team having a passion to create a superior dining experience. Apparently they have a lot of people who like it. But, I knew something was up when they didn't bring a bill."

"What was up?"

"Tell you in a minute, but can I tell you about the restaurant name first?"

"Sure. I'm intrigued."

"Well, Rick, the head chef, knows ABS, and when he sat down at our table I asked about the name. He told me the whole story. I'll see if I can remember everything. Rick says the way to pronounce it is, "Caribsea" all one word. It's named after a World War II merchant ship that was torpedoed by a German U Boat in 1943. The Caribsea was hauling war fighting materials to Norfolk from Cuba and decided to leave the convoy which was protecting it. The ship's captain wanted to make sure he was on time. That decision cost his ship, its cargo, and most of his crew. Twenty-eight of the thirty-five men died."

"What a terrible name for a restaurant then!"

"Hang on Mom. What's cool is how they merge North Carolina coastal history and regional building material throughout the restaurant. For example, the elevator rises in the center of the building like it is the ship's boiler room, which is where the first torpedo struck. The sign on the building and even their menus have a tiger shark on it because about fifty tiger sharks guard the ship's graveyard at the bottom of the Atlantic. Many divers like to visit it. Rick and ABS have even dived it, together. One cool story Rick told is about a man who lived near Ocracoke, on the Outer Banks. During the war, the man was walking along the coastline early one morning when he came upon a plank of wood which he threw back into the water. The tide kept pushing it back toward him. On the third or fourth time, the man turned it over and sadly discovered it was from his son's ship, the Caribsea. He knew then his son was lost at sea.

Rick is really proud of his restaurant. He went on and on about how they decorate with regional art work and constructed their walls with reclaimed North Carolina barn wood. The dark ceiling, which shows exposed pipes, carries the ship theme throughout the restaurant."

"How neat. That sounds better. How about food? What did you eat?"

"I had the Caribsea burger with fries and ABS had the gourmet grilled cheese. I wasn't really too hungry. For my drink I tried an Arnold Palmer. Sounds like alcohol Mom, but it's really half lemonade and half sweet tea. It was delicious! They have lots of choices I'm sure you would like. I asked Rick what he recommends as his favorite dish. He quickly said, "Shrimp and Grits." Rick has a Charleston trained sous chef who developed his own unique version. I bet Grandpa would enjoy it. Another thing I learned is their special drinks are named in honor of the ship's sinking. They have one drink called the SS Diver and they also have local names like Bogue Sound Melon. Another interesting drink is called "Loose Lips Sink Ships". This name comes from the fact that during the early part of World War II, sailors and civilians did not think about what they were saying or writing and some-times accidentally gave away their ships' positions. This may have happened to the Caribsea. Rick told me that during the war the government had a huge advertising campaign to remind Americans that spies are everywhere and to be careful. Anyway, it was so cool to go with ABS. I think we should go back sometime."

"That sounds fun. Maybe we can take the entire fam-ily to celebrate our new home. Maybe ABS can come too."

"Well Mom, about that. I'm pretty sure he can be there since he owns part of it. ABS and a couple other guys are partners."

"Seriously Journey? You didn't misunderstand? ABS owns part of CaribSea?"

"Yep. I didn't misunderstand. Who would have ever thought? ABS isn't very old and look at the beat up truck he drives. But then you told me about his boat and I got to ride on his motorcycle. I guess he's full of surprises. And remember, you told me once to never judge a book by its cover. Oh yeah, ABS said to tell you he'll see you tomorrow. He has to work on a few things before the weekend is over."

Hmmm. This man is full of surprises. Maybe I can surprise him, too.

"Journey. I'm glad you had a great time. The turtle walk sounds exciting, probably more than you thought it would be. And it sounds like going to the fort might be something to do this summer and next. I'd love to see the Civil War reenactment. Wasn't it nice of ABS to do this for you? Now, with all the talk about food, I'm feeling a little hungry. Would you help me with the umbrella please so we can go eat? Grandpa's cooking steaks!"

As we walk up the path, my cell rings again. This time it's Crutch.

"Go ahead Journey, while I take this call."

"Hi, Kirby," Crutch said excitedly, as if we had a long time relationship. "How are you? I was wondering if you might like to drive to Wilmington for dinner and a movie tomorrow night. I have a three-day layover."

"Crutch, I thought I made it clear last time we spoke. I really don't have an interest in a relationship right now." With you, I wanted to add.

. . .

"No, I don't think you do understand. I'm sorry, but I wish you would stop calling."

. . .

"No, I won't just give you a second chance. There wasn't even a first chance."

...

"Yeah. If something changes, I promise I'll call you. But for now, please stop calling."

Weird! Wonder if this is what it feels like to be stalked. I don't want to alarm anyone, but this is creepy.

"Hang on. I'll catch you," I yell to Journey, racing up the dunes.

Chapter 20

Cat's Surprise

What a great day this has been - other than a few hang up calls. Sometimes it seems there is no one on the other end, while other times it feels like someone is watching me answer the phone. And I can't get creepy Crutch's call out of my mind.

Unfortunately, I can't talk to anyone about it. Dad and ABS would probably go half-cocked and get into trouble. Journey is too young to understand, and Grams and Mom want me to "get back in the saddle" so they will probably like that I have another suitor. Is that what you call it? It's been so long since I even thought of dating one man, much less two. Well, I told him "no" and that's final.

So, what's a young widow to do on a Saturday evening? What a morbid thought. Try it again Kirby. Okay, what's a single girl to do on a Saturday evening? Much better!

I think about cuddling up in my room and catching up on some television or a good romance novel. It's been a long time since I did either. The middle of summer is the worst time for watching tv and I don't have a book.

The Olympics don't start for another week and all the shows are reruns. It just might be a good time to take a stroll down the beach and surprise ABS. I really want to thank him for being so kind to Journey. I haven't seen him this excited in a long time. And, I'm sort of excited too.

Journey said ABS would see me tomorrow, but why wait?

Fixing my sun bleached hair – it sure is getting long which helps me look younger - I throw on the blue and white Dakota jumpsuit I picked up in Beaufort a few weeks ago. Fits like a glove and shows just enough skin without being too, what's the word, provocative.

Bumping into Mom on the way out I say, "Just running a few errands." I wonder if she can tell I'm headed toward the beach and not my car - which is why she answers my thought by yelling, "Tell ABS hello." She knows he lives down the beach.

How do she and Grams always know what I'm thinking? Luckily, that pain *Karma* has not been lurking around recently, unless you count Crutch as one of her minions. God, I hope not! "Be back in a little bit," I say to no one in particular, as I skip around the pool to the path.

Dinner was great and this walk is perfect for burning off the extra calories Dad put into the steak and potatoes. I told him I wanted a fat free steak! Anyway, the sun is just about to dip below the purple and gold horizon. White caps dance as the dark blue waves roll in with slow regularity. Just like earlier today, it was perfect for rafting or floating in the surf like Grams and Aunt Reagan do so easily.

The sand under my bare feet has turned cool, which is amazing given they burned when I ran through the sand just a few hours ago. I quickly pass a young couple walking arm in arm obviously content in their own thoughts as they splash through the waves without acknowledging me. Families busily wrap up their day in the sun, taking canopies down and dragging lawn chairs and boogie boards to the top of the dunes to wait for another day. Fishermen with hopes of filling buckets for a late dinner, or at least catching bait fish to try again in the morning, replace them. One of them looks at me a little too long and says, "How ya doin?" to which I reply, "Super," as I walk away. And, I realize, I actually am. *Super.* I feel like I'm walking on top of the waves, headed to surprise one of the nicest, most gorgeous, and honest men I know, who seems to have an interest in me. What could be better? I guess I'm back in the saddle, Grams.

The Trav-L-Park is only about a mile down the beach. I spot the park's beach access sign, climb the winding boardwalk over the dunes, and begin looking for his trailer. I can hear the popular East Coast band, Spare Change, playing slow moving beach music in the background, at the same gazebo we used a few weeks ago. I remember ABS said he's owned the trailer a long time, but he never told me where it is. Come to think of it, that's sort of interesting. I know it's in the front. But, is the beach at the front or back of a travel park? I haven't a clue and decide to ask the nearby teenage girls, wearing bikini tops and shorts that should be illegal in public. They're about Journey's age, I guess. Living at the beach, I better get ready for dealing with girls like this.

"Excuse me. Can you tell me where ABS' trailer is?"

Smirks and muffled laughter tell me they know. Of course they do. How stupid can I be? He is, after all, probably the hottest single man in the park, and they are hormonal young women.

"Well, can you?" I ask again, with a little hint of attitude.

"Sure, ma'am."

Ouch. I probably deserved the "ma'am" because of my snippiness.

"It's right around the corner to your right. Sits up high on the dune with a great view. Ya can't miss it."

"Thanks," I manage to offer, a bit weaker than I meant. How do they know he has a great view? Seems like they know a bit more than someone their age should.

"You're welcome, ma'am. Have a nice evening," the taller girl said her words dripping with sarcasm.

Could it be jealousy or my imagination?

Gathering myself, I head down the road. Man, wish I had worn sandals. This concrete path in the park is rocky. The pebbles are big enough to hurt but small enough to not see.

Focus, I remind myself. *Keep your eyes on the prize. I'm headed to see a wonderful man!*

As I crest the top of a long ago paved-over sand dune, I hear the sound of a woman moaning or perhaps crying softly--almost whimpering. Then I hear another voice whispering, sounding strangely familiar. It's faint and I can't understand everything. Not wanting to be intruding, I consider walking away. As I start to turn, I hear it clearer.

"ABS, I can't believe it. What will I do? How will I survive? This is all I have. I've been with you for nearly a year. I can't believe this. Can't you fix it?"

ABS? Did I hear that right?

Is this what he had to take care of? Why he couldn't see me until tomorrow? I edge closer, standing in the shadow of another recreational vehicle.

Now I clearly hear ABS.

"Cat, I'm so sorry. Things are out of my control. I care deeply for you, but I just can't. You're one of the most important people in my life. You know I'll do whatever I can to get you on your feet. But right now, you just can't stay."

...Care deeply... Can't stay.

Oh my God. I've heard enough. This is why he couldn't see me until tomorrow. He has to get rid of this bimbo. Nearly fainting, my head swims. Stumbling as I leave, I hear ABS call out, "Who's there?"

I want to yell out and confront him. Instead, I begin to run. Blindly, the salty tears sting my eyes and my rubbery legs are worthless. My heart is broken, yet again. Unfortunately, this one is still alive. How can he do this? I hate him! He spent all day with my son. What a liar. Running down the slope near the park's beach access, I hear the same teenage tarts say, "That didn't take long," followed by something obscene and high-pitched laughter.

I got back on the saddle Grams, but the saddle slipped under the horse!

Half-running, half-falling down the beach toward home, I hear the same fishermen yell something unintelligible, while a few caring beach goers ask, "Are you okay?"

I can't stop - have to get away. I can deal with a man who breaks my heart saving thousands of people by ditching his experimental plane. But not this. I can't do this.

Arriving home, I race to my room and launch myself onto the bed. The surf has ruined my outfit and my Medusa-like hair wraps around my head. Tear-thinned mascara found every wrinkle this thirty-something face has hidden. Of course, he would want one of the younger women. I saw her. Cat, that's what he called her. She even has a cool name. Not Kirby, like an old fashioned vacuum. Petite, blonde, high cheek bones and a European accent. I can't compete.

Suddenly, I know exactly what to do. Taking deep breaths, I compose myself and think about what to say. I pick up the phone, dial, and wait for an answer.

Chapter 21

Wilmington Mickey

"Hi Crutch. It's Kirby."

...

"Yes, I know. I'm as surprised as you! Well, I've given it some thought and wonder if the offer is still good for tomorrow?"

...

"Tonight? Thank you. But, no. I'd like to, but I really need some sleep. What shall I bring?"

...

"That's sweet Crutch, but I'll pack a few more things than my toothbrush."

...

"Baseball game at one? Sure. Sounds fun. I used to live at Topsail and I know where the stadium is. I'll meet you at the game."

...

"Sure. Dinner afterwards sound nice. I'll see you tomorrow."

...

"You sleep well, too. Good night Crutch."

Falling back on the bed, as soon as I press the button to disconnect I think, *Crap, what have I done?* Too late now. He seems a little bit weird, but at least he's interested in *me*! As I turn my face into my pillow, I accept tonight won't be the first time in the past year I've cried myself to sleep.

I wake up early. I need to get off this island, quickly and quietly. After scrubbing my face and drying my sniffles, I cuddle with Journey and lie through my teeth. I never did this before, but I can't ruin what he thinks of ABS. Even if ABS is a liar and a cheat. I jot a short note for Mom and Dad thanking them in advance for watching Journey, saying I'm headed to visit friends in Wilmington. Wilmington's only ninety minutes away and I plan to be back later tonight or maybe the next day. I'll call and let them know. It's sort of true. I do have high school friends in Hampstead, Holly Ridge, and Topsail. Maybe someone even moved to Wilmington. Anyway, I just ABSOLUTELY need some time away from all of this! And I don't want anyone to worry about me. I'm a big girl!

After sweetly kissing Journey on his forehead and silently inching my way down the stairs, I make it to the car. I wonder how I am going to turn this hotrod on without waking everyone. Suddenly, this isn't an issue as Dad is standing there, beside my car.

"Hey Baby, where are you headed off to this early?"

"Oh, hi Dad. I left a note on the kitchen counter."

"Got it. I also thought I heard someone crying last night. Just sort of thinking out loud and wonder if you have anything you want to share with your *favorite* dad."

Ironic word choice I thought, given my experience with ducking serious issues and driving off the bridge! That time I found out Brooks really isn't my father... I sure can't say anything about that -- not now. We've come so far in our relationship since then, twenty-some years ago.

"Sorry Dad. I just got lonely and need some time away. I can't really explain it but, well, you know when things are screwed up in your head sometimes you can clear it by getting away? That's where I am right now."

"Okay, Baby Girl. Mom and I trust and love you. We'll take care of Journey, although he's almost a man and doesn't need much looking after. Anything I need to know about? Your house, ABS, anything?"

Man, this hurt! They trust me and I'm lying to his face. Well, I'm just not telling him everything.

"Thanks so much Dad. I'm good. I'll let you know what's going on and when I'll be back. Won't be long. Love you all too!"

Opening the car door, he says, "Whatever's troubling you will blow over. Hang in there and be safe. Call me if you need anything!"

I fight back tears as he bends over and kisses my forehead, as I had Journey's minutes ago. "Thanks Dad. Love you."

I hate myself for lying to nearly everyone in my immediate family. Grams is not up this early, or I would have been sunk! She knows me too well.

Cruising toward Wilmington, I review my plan. So, here's the deal, Kirby:

Put some time and distance behind you and see what happens. Sure, ABS is a two-timing jerk and doesn't deserve you. Just go check out this other guy. I promised myself, and now Dad, that I would be safe, but you just never know for sure. Remember all the crazy phone calls and hang ups? And, Crutch has popped up at really odd times - like after the memorial service. Okay, stop talking to yourself and think about other things.

"Oh no," I groan as soon as I turn on the radio blaring lyrics to one of Pappy's old favorites, "Another Saturday Night and I Ain't Got Nobody." Seriously, what else could have possibly been playing? Maybe I can scan the "Oldies but Goodies" stations and find another stick-in-the-eye song to make me feel better. How about something from Elvis? Maybe, "Are you Lonesome Tonight?" Or, perhaps I'll hear Celine's rendition of "All by Myself." I've always believed in omens and as soon as I figure this one out I'll take action. For now, "click" is the answer.

Tooling along, with the rest of the early birds headed south, I have the top down with the warming late summer sun rising to my right. If I wasn't so mad, I'd be happy. There's only one thing to do. I decide to, in the words of my Yankee friends, "fuhgeddaboudit." Phew; that's better. Now I'm ready for some fun. If it really is so easy. New River Air Station to my left reminds me of some of my old haunts. Holly Ridge and Hampstead flow right into each other now, like Swannsboro, Cedar Point, and Cape Carteret, closer to Emerald Isle. The entire area has grown up so much since I lived here. Pushing my muscle car's speedometer past seventy, we're almost floating. Blue lights behind me quickly bring me back to earth. As fast as I was going, they might put me under the jail. But, no. He races right by. *Thank you Lord*, I pray silently. There's my omen. Everything's going to be okay.

I still slow way down. I'd rather get stopped for going too slow for the next thirty minutes. And what's the rush anyway? Game starts at one o'clock. Slowing to a near crawl, I'm much more aware of my surroundings and realize I'm only a few minutes from the stadium. I peek at my phone and see I've missed several calls from ABS. I hit the return call button and quickly cancel, before it connects. Then, I punch in his number, but don't hit send. Nope, not giving in, even though his message says he wants to see me and wonders why I took off without talking to him. "I'm worried," he texts adding, "Be safe." Obviously, he spoke with Dad. I don't care. He made his bed...

With more than hour to spare, I head over to Mayfaire Town Center. It's new since we lived here, and I've been dying to have a reason to visit. *Man, I could stay here all day*, I think as I scan the eclectic mix of stores and restaurants. Perhaps I can get Crutch to come back here for dinner – and of course we could visit some shops. Gap, Banana Republic, Bevello, Francesca's – they're all here. It sure would be nice to live closer.

It was fun window shopping. Now I know where to eat, unless Crutch already has plans. I drive around the stadium parking lot in search of the right space. Mom always laughs at me as I will run for an hour without complaint but take ten minutes to find the closest and best parking spot. Dad taught me right. Half the battle is to make sure no one will ding my brand new car. There appears to be a fairly large crowd for a summertime Sunday afternoon game. I feel the excitement in the air and then see why. Several New York Yankees are here signing autographs and scouting their farm team players. *Too cool*, I think, wishing Journey could be here. Maybe we'll come back if this turns out okay.

"Hi Crutch," I yell across several car tops when I see him walking toward me. I wonder how he knew where I parked? He has never seen my new car. Interesting question to ask when the time is right.

"Hi yourself," he replies, moving in for a clumsy hug, ignoring my hand. "Glad you're early. The stadium is packed since some of the Yankees are here. Want an autograph before we get something to eat?"

Thomas P. Gill

"No, actually I'm famished. I left early and drove around a bit, but didn't get anything to eat. Nothing better than a ball game dog with everything on it."

"You bet. Although don't get too full. We'll have a nice dinner, too."

Taking my hand, Crutch guides me through the ticket taker turnstile. We have awesome seats, right behind home plate, so we can see all the action. Then again, Legion Stadium's Buck Hardee Field has no bad seats. Through the first few innings, Crutch is a perfect gentleman. Drinks, food, and conversation are perfect. He says he really loves kids and wants some, eventually.

While definitely a southern girl, I don't glisten when it's near one hundred degrees, in the shade. I sweat! Even wearing shorts and a baseball game appropriate tank top, I'm soaked.

"Kirby, can I get you a ball cap or maybe I can get seats up in the bleachers where there's some shade?"

Looking around at other fans, some of who are now shirtless or fanning themselves violently with their programs, I say, "How sweet, Crutch. But when I'm this hot the only thing that really works is to get into water or air conditioning. I usually only sweat like this when there's no breeze at the beach. I'm not even this soaked when I take a shower."

"Got it. How about we go for a ride or a swim at the pool or beach?"

"Sure. That sounds harmless. I love the game, but it's just too hot. I'd hate to be the players."

When we get to our cars, Crutch offers to follow me to his hotel. He even plugged the Riverfront Hilton address into my phone GPS. Bells go off, but I have to do something with my car. "Sure," I agree again, with a bit of trepidation.

The trip downtown to the hotel will be short, so I leave my convertible top up. I feel the air conditioning immediately. "Ahh," I moan with no one to hear me. It sure feels better. Glancing down at my phone, I see I missed several more calls. One is from my dad and many more from ABS.

"Hi Dad," I say as he answers my return call. "Sure, everything's fine. I just left a baseball game and am headed to a friend's place." *All true.*

...

"ABS? Yes. I see he called, a bunch of times."

...

"Really? I don't know exactly what he's talking about. Did you tell him where I went?"

...

"Dad, I really don't want to discuss this right now. I'm disappointed in something he did, but hope you will keep that confidential. I just need some time. If I need anything, I'll call you. Okay?"

...

"Thanks Dad. I know you understand, even if you don't really know what's going on. Love you! See you soon."

So, ABS is worried and cares. At least someone does. Frankly, I don't give a... Well, Mom says don't say anything if you can't say something nice. And right now there is a very handsome, former military pilot, who appears to have an interest in me, standing at my car door.

"A bird in the hand" moment.

Waiting patiently, Crutch asks, "Everything okay, Kirby? You look a little upset."

"No, nothing wrong Crutch. Just talking with my dad. Thanks for asking. Is it okay to park here?"

"Absolutely fine. It's out of the way, and no one can see it to mess with it."

Second omen: he cares about my car -- that means a lot to me!

"Great, well what shall we do?"

"How about a night cap?"

"Ha ha, it's only three o'clock. I think you have a long time before that happens." *Maybe never*, I think to myself, if he's asking about a night cap in the middle of the afternoon.

"It's five o'clock somewhere," he laughs using the tired old Jimmy Buffet line.

"Just not here," I retort.

"Good one. So, how about we go for a walk along the river. Then we can drive over to Mayfaire and eat at Tokyo 101. Okay with you?"

"That sounds great. I saw it earlier today and hoped I might persuade you to take me there. How did you know?"

How did he know? Was he watching me drive around Mayfaire? I did park in front of that very restaurant for a pretty long time checking my phone and makeup. Something is not adding up. I'm getting that same creepy feeling I had when Crutch showed up unannounced at Sam's memorial service.

"Just lucky, I guess."

"Okay. Just give me a minute. I'll be right out."

Closing the car door, I quickly call Dad back and quietly leave a voice message. "Hi Dad, just wanted you to know I'm okay but something feels a little strange with the friend I'm with. I'm okay, but please just keep your phone handy."

"Okay, let's go," I say, wanting to give Crutch the benefit of the doubt. He really does seem like a caring guy. And, he is easy on the eyes, for sure!

I'm amazed at the recently renovated Riverwalk as we stroll carelessly along the river. I haven't been here in years. It's obvious someone has been pouring money into this part of town.

"Wow, this is beautiful," I exclaim. "They've done such a nice job of making a walking, strolling, and jogging path. I'm sure it's to get the tourists to spend more money. Emerald Isle could do something like this. Sure, we have the Plantation, but we could do more near the pier."

"It is very nice," he replies, reaching down to hold my hand as we cross the intersection.

Pulling my hand to my side I say, "I'm fine Crutch. It's a bit early," I add, wanting him to realize I'm setting the boundaries.

"Sorry, Kirby. I'll take it slower."

"Thanks. I came to get to know you and enjoy the company. Please don't ruin it."

"You bet. Slow and steady wins the race."

Not racing here bud, I wanted to say, but bit my tongue. *After all*, I called him and came of my own volition. I need to be nice to him, for now.

Our walk was enjoyable. While I'm still sweating in this oppressive heat, at least the air conditioning and ice cold lemonade at Elijah's, just off the river on Ann Street, cool us down a bit. Now, not far from where we began, Crutch suggests we get ready for dinner.

"Hey Kirby, how about we try The Pilot House for dinner, instead of Tokyo 101? Then we won't need to move either car for dinner. We could try it another time, if that works for you."

I'm a little disappointed to not go to Mayfaire, but it seems to make sense. I agree.

"Need to freshen up before dinner?" Crutch asks.

"That would be great. Thanks."

"Great. We can use my room, and then walk down to dinner. It's just a few blocks from the hotel."

Well, where else would I freshen up? But, then, I'm not even sure I'm spending the night in Wilmington. And he doesn't know if I plan to stay with a friend or head home after dinner. It's okay. I just need to be careful.

Once in his hotel room, Crutch says, "You go first, I'll wait."

"Okay, I'll just be a few minutes."

Having retrieved a dress from my car, I make a fast change to look more presentable for dinner. I brush through my hair and apply just a touch of makeup, because I don't want to encourage him. I'm going to, not becoming, dinner.

As I come out of the bathroom, Crutch is standing beside the door, as if he might have been listening or possibly looking in.

"Humph," I clear my throat as if to ask if he needs help with something. He breezes by without an apparent care in the world. Maybe I'm reading into it. Maybe not.

Regardless, I slip my hand into my purse and check my phone. It's on. Good, I have plenty of charge, too. Just in case. And, of course, there are several more missed calls from you guessed it, ABS.

Sorry, you snooze, you lose. Or more appropriately, *you cheat, you're beat!* But it does feel good to see how many times he's called.

It's refreshing walking down the boardwalk toward the restaurant. The sun is long into its daily descent. The steady breeze off the river, accompanying the shade from the towering oaks along the path, offer relief that would have been more welcome hours earlier. The cobblestone path in this historic section of town is reminiscent of other North Carolina waterfront towns, like Swansboro and Elizabeth City. Smaller yachts and pleasure boats are tied up beside the restaurants allowing boaters to cruise right to dinner. This is what I call a real drive-in.

"Hey Crutch, have you ever toured the USS North Carolina," I ask, as we look across the Cape Fear river at the looming World War Two era battleship, moored in Wilmington since before I was born.

"I haven't, but I spent months on several others during my time in the military."

"Sorry. I sort of forgot about that. We always enjoyed touring the battleship when I was a kid. I discovered something new every time. I would never have lasted living in those cramped quarters."

With a coy smile he says, "Nah. You would have been **just** fine. But, you would have caused quite a stir among all the men on board. And..., here we are. Let me get the door," he offers as we arrive, right on time for our dinner reservation.

I don't know when, but I guess he called ahead.

The dinner was great with perfect presentation, taste, and a tourist-town ambiance, which makes me feel like I'm on vacation, even when just a short drive from home. My shrimp and crab corn chowder was delicious, and the sesame seared tuna was so filling, I'm not sure I can even walk back to the hotel.

Crutch excused himself to the restroom, allowing me to reflect on the day and evening.

So far, Crutch has been almost a complete gentleman. Perhaps I've read him wrong. A baseball game, Riverwalk stroll, and now a fancy dinner, with only an occasional inappropriate comment or two, like a night cap in the middle of the afternoon. We are adults after all -- nearly forty years old. Did I just think that - pushing forty? Is that even possible?

Anyway, I excuse myself when Crutch returns. I quickly check my phone in the restroom and see ABS has called again. Not once. At least five more times. I don't have the desire to check the messages. He can worry, if he is. He gets what he deserves.

Crutch took the liberty to order after-dinner cocktails, which are waiting at the table. "Hi, good looking. I ordered a martini for myself and the Ocean Drive for you. I hope you don't mind. If I'm not mistaken, you like Malibu Coconut Rum. This one adds a twist of Blue Curacao with just enough orange, pineapple, and cranberry juice to make you feel like you're on a tropical island."

"I'm not sure this is a good idea. I don't drink...," I start. But then, why not? "Well, okay. Just this one. But, I've got to be heading home in just a little bit."

"Sounds good and I'll make sure you get to bed in one piece. Enjoy."

That sounds weird, but what can it hurt? I think I find out a few minutes later.

"Crutch, you are sooo right! This drink is awesom-mme. It's delicious and it tastes good, too."

I think I'm slurring my words and saying things that don't make sense, but he doesn't seem to notice.

"I can taste the island and smell the pineapple. Thank you! You are really special, Crutch. I think I like you."

Pretty soon I feel like I'm flying. Crutch seems to be helping me up from the table and escorting me outside.

"She's okay," I hear him telling people, as we walk out. "We've been going all day and I think the drink may have gotten the best of her. We'll get some fresh air and head back to our hotel."

If I hadn't eaten dinner, I'd swear I'm drunk. I only had one drink, but alcohol and I don't mix well, especially on an empty stomach. Then again, I'm stuffed. And, I didn't even finish the drink. My head is spinning, but I'm pretty sure I heard, "our hotel."

"Heyyy friends. Waitttt just a minute, or an hour," I mumble to the couple getting ready to enter the restaurant. They ignore me.

"Come on darlin'. You just need some fresh air."

"I'm not your darling," I yell as I swing and miss, while he grabs my wrists.

Outside, the fresh air wakes me up a little and I fumble in my purse for my phone.

"Kirby, just relax and come with me. It'll be okay. I'll take good care of you. I promise. I know what you need."

I do too.

Crutch's right hand clamps tightly around the back of my neck as he whispers in my left ear, "Don't say a word! Just do what I tell you to."

That woke me up. Unable to call out with my voice, I realize I might be able to call with my phone. Refreshed more, as the cool air hits my face, I hit my recent calls button and hope someone listens.

"Crutch," I begin. "Don't hurt me. I'll do anything you want. You don't have to be mean. Didn't we have a good time today?"

"Hush," he hisses, forcefully propelling me down the cobblestone towards the hotel.

"What did you do? Did you put a mickey in my drink? You didn't have to do that Crutch. I'll do anything for you. Are we going back to the Hilton? It sure is pretty down here by the river."

Oh my God, I've heard of women being taken advantage of at bars, but not me. No way this is happening.

"Shut up! I know you'll do whatever I want. I've wanted you since I met you on my plane. I've tried to get your attention so many times. Now I have it. Don't I?"

I don't have a clue how we got to the elevator. I'm barely able to stand, so Crutch places both hands around my waist to keep me from falling. I'm sure I look like a tramp who can't hold her liquor.

Can't anyone see I need help? I don't dare scream. With his hand twisting my arm behind me there's no telling what he might do or say, now or later.

The elevator stops at the second floor. An elderly couple enters and, as expected, they don't even look in my direction, at first. Three, Four, Five, Six, Seven floors. Finally, on the ninth floor, the elevator stops. The doors open. But it's only the elderly couple getting off. For the past few floors they were sneaking ugly glares. If only I could have risked getting their attention.

Crutch quickly presses the button and the doors close.

It's all over now. One more floor, and no one to help me. Then what? How? Why did I get into this mess?

Ding, the elevator bell rings once more. Time's up. If I had only...

The doors slowly open. Suddenly, Crutch is snatched from me like candy from a baby. I stumble to the floor. My left leg splays out and keeps the door from closing. It continues to bump against me every few seconds as I hear fists pounding skin. I can't even lift my head. As my cheek lays against the cool elevator floor, I only imagine what is happening. Finally, I hear someone calling my name. Softly at first and then, "KIRBY, IT'S ME, ABS. I've got you. You're safe!"

Lifting me to him in one effortless motion, ABS nestles me to his chest with his bulging biceps. I glance down the hallway. Even in my stupor, I make out the beaten, bloodied mass that used to be Crutch's face. My stomach can't take it and I lose my dinner. ABS rips off his shirt and delicately cleans my face. He holds me close as we descend the ten floors that minutes ago were my stairway to hell.

ABS motions to the lobby rent-a-cop with a nod of his head and says, "Tenth floor..., need a cleanup. And an ambulance."

Hours later, we lay in another room as the fog swirling in my brain begins to dissipate. I hear the unmistakable ocean roar and sense I'm at Emerald Isle.

"Hey baby. It's so good to see you back in the world. That jerk gave you something strong. You've been out most of the morning. But, he won't bother you again. I promise!"

"ABS, thanks! But, how did you find me?"

"Your dad told me. After twenty calls, he finally said you went to Wilmington to see Crutch. I still don't know why. I sensed he was up to no good and you are just too innocent and naive. On the way to Wilmington, I found out what hotel he was staying in by checking with the airlines. They wouldn't tell me his hotel, but they did tell me the hotel chains their flight crews normally use. Thankfully, I guessed right. I didn't know for sure, until you called me back. That was brilliant!"

"Brilliant? I don't think so. I was just hoping someone would come rescue me...and you did! But ABS, we still need to talk."

"We do sweetheart. I need to know why you ran off and spent the day, and what could have been the night, with another man. What did I do?"

"Exactly. What did you do? Let me tell you!" I could feel my blood pressure rising and my head is starting to pound again.

"I walked down the beach to surprise you at your trailer Saturday night. I guess maybe this trailer. I was so excited because Journey had such a great day with you. Anyway, I saw you."

"Saw me? What are you talking about?"

"Cat. I saw you holding her and telling her it will be okay. I couldn't hear everything, but you said something about needing more time. She's so young and pretty. ABS, I can't blame you. But, I couldn't believe what I was hearing and just had to get away. Crutch had been asking to get together for months, so I called him. I didn't want to, but I was just so mad at you! And, I still am."

"Seriously Kirby? Listen to me. Cat is short for Kateryna. She is a Ukrainian mixologist at my restaurant bar. You know, Caribsea. I'm sure Journey told you about it, as I was going to tomorrow. Anyway, she just found out her work visa has been pulled for some stupid irregularity. She has to go back home for at least six months before she can reapply. Nine Eleven made it difficult for aliens to remain in America. Even with the smallest issue, legal aliens can be sent home and worry about being able to return. Nothing more than that. Kat is very special to me, to all of us. Her father and grandfather were world-class mixologists, too. And she is a sweet young lady! We're lucky to have her here and I'll do almost anything to get her back. But Kirby, she means nothing to me as a woman! Nothing! You have to believe me."

I see and hear it. ABS is sincere and I'm so sorry. How could I have acted so immature?

"Oh ABS. How could I have been so stupid? I was just so jealous and couldn't believe what I heard. She is so cute and young and I'm... well, you know, old."

"That's crap and you know it. Kirby, I've loved you since the day we met. What can I do or say to make you understand? Age is just a number! Do you believe in love at first sight?"

"I do ABS. I do and promise I won't be so stupid again. It's been difficult for the past months, and well, I'll just have to believe you from now on. Will you forgive me?"

As he pulls me close, I feel his racing heart and know he's beginning to forgive me.

Chapter 22

The Storm

The past few weeks have been incredibly busy. Once we got home, I shared with Mom and Dad about Crutch and apologized for how thoughtless I had been. Together, we decided to not press charges. ABS had pressed enough of Crutch's face into the hotel floor that he won't mess with me, or anyone else, again. I came clean with Journey, too.

"No secrets between us ever again, I promise," I told him through my tear stained eyes. Once again, he is so understanding. Just like his father!

With summer's end fast approaching, we are preparing for the move to our new beach house. Journey said, "If I can have the room with the balcony overlooking the ocean I agree to everything else."

That's easy enough since I was giving him that room, anyway. He's been such a trooper this past year. Now he's fully engaged patrolling with ABS on Saturday turtle walks and spends two days a week at Fort Macon. Dad committed to drive his only grandson to the fort until we move to Atlantic Beach. Since it's only a few miles further, he'll be able to ride his scooter, eventually. He's already spent time with the park rangers to ensure he knows what to tell people about the turtles. He even set up a small booth near the three nests.

Thankfully, the nests are all fairly close together on the eastern end of the island where the ocean mixes with the sound. It's rough water and very few tourists or locals venture that far. The rip tides are so severe that few go in the water at the point. He sometimes catches visitors as they take the boardwalk to the sunbathing and picnic area. Several tourists have complimented Journey's turtle knowledge to the park superintendent. They are amazed to learn he's only fourteen. I know how much he has learned as I have the *pleasure* of listening to all of his speeches. At least he's not getting into trouble, like his mom.

In the meantime, Grams, Mom, and I have been busy deciding on which furniture to keep from my military shipment and what to buy new. I'm with Grams who suggested, "get rid of everything and start fresh." It has been great to have her back. Grams has not had to start dialysis treatments. Her blood tests show her kidneys are returning to normal. Diet control will be the primary prescription, although, with her cooking, that can present a problem all of its own.

Today we're looking for bargains or, as Dad says, "saving money" at Shore Décor in Morehead City. Our new beach house came fully furnished and the bedrooms were tastefully decorated, so I'm really looking for nautical theme accessories.

"Hey Mom," I ask, "Did you hear Hurricane Michele's headed our way? They say it could hit between Miami and Norfolk sometime this Saturday, right during our ECU football game and move-in party. What luck!"

"First world problem, Baby Girl," she replies. "At least you're moving into a beach house. I heard something about the storm yesterday, but we still have a few days before it becomes anything serious. We can watch the news, and if necessary, move the party inside."

Grams adds, "Honey, you know we don't have hurricanes on Emerald Isle. On Bogue Banks, either. I've been here almost thirty years and never had more than a Cat Two. And we clean those up in thirty minutes."

"I hope so Grams. We've got about fifty people coming."

We found some fantastic deals on lamps and wall hangings – exactly what we need to pull the rooms together. And this late in the season, we landed some outstanding deals on outside deck furniture at bargain prices. But, I didn't appreciate the "Hurricane Sale - 25% off" sign. I do believe in omens.

Two days later, the forecast is gloomier. Michele has become a massive storm and is threatening the entire east coast. All the national weather channels have adjusted their spaghetti storm tracks to an expected landing between Cape Fear and Morehead City. Outliers predict it could land anywhere between Savannah, Georgia and Richmond, Virginia. It seems like meteorologists throw darts and hope one lands in the bulls eye.

Already a Category Two storm, they expect it to become a Category Three before tomorrow. Michele blew through the Dominican Republic and portions of Cuba causing massive damage as she ripped across villages and resorts. Hundreds of people are dead. The Florida governor ordered a mandatory evacuation from the Keys to Jacksonville for anyone within fifty miles of the coast. Obviously, politicians and police agencies learned a few things from Katrina. Governors and emergency management teams watch television updates and hold their breath.

"Mom, what are we going to do?" Journey asks. "We have all these people coming in two days. I got the storm tracker guide out so we can get our supplies. Here's the list of what we need. Batteries, water, propane for the grill, matches, and a bunch of other stuff. Want to drive over to Ace Hardware and Food Lion to stock up?"

"Good idea, Journey. I think we'll cancel or, rather, postpone the celebration for now. And we can go to get supplies before the rush. I'll call ABS and Mom to see if they need anything."

Seems like we may be the least prepared people on the island. The stores' shelves are practically empty. I should have been a Girl Scout. Maybe I would have remembered to, "Be Prepared." At least we got a couple cases of water and some radio batteries. We picked up propane at ACE

Hardware so we can cook out, if needed. ABS came by later in the day to check on us. He had visited with Mom and Dad. They're fine. He said he'd would come out to-morrow and weather the storm with us, unless it turns into a Cat Four, in which case we all need to evacuate.

Glued to the television, with less than thirty-six hours before the storm's predicted landfall, I postpone the party. Now a full blown Cat Three hurricane, with sustained winds of over one hundred and twenty-five miles per hour, Michele packs a punch. All aircraft at the nearby Marine Air bases have been relocated inland or up the coast. Colleges, schools, and non-emergency medical clinics are closed. The North Carolina governor followed Florida's lead and declared a state of emergency, relaxing rules allowing farmers to harvest their fields before it's too late. This is getting scary!

Meteorologists and news anchors update continuously, which thankfully overshadows the election year ongoing political banter, as Michele regains strength over the warm open Atlantic. She glances off the Miami coast and, after skirting out to sea just close enough to scare Savannah, is now headed directly for North Carolina. With expected wind gusts exceeding one hundred and forty-five miles per hour, Michele is a killer storm barreling directly for us, islanders and coastal Carolinians.

Last night, the North Carolina barrier island mayors of Emerald Isle, Atlantic Beach, Indian Beach, Salter Path, and Pine Knoll Shores issued voluntary evacuations ahead of the expected landfall. The Coast Guard station battened their hatches and television stations scroll messages repeatedly stating rescue missions will cease until after the storm. The Governor followed, requesting non-essential people evacuate as soon as possible. Sirens sound continuously and emergency vehicles drive slowly through residential areas and on flood prone roads blaring announcements:

Voluntary evacuation is in effect immediately. Evacuate by three o'clock tomorrow. There will be no emergency service during the storm. You will be unable to leave or return to the island until the curfew is lifted.

Having watched television news updates relentlessly through the night, I call Mom at seven o'clock.

"Hi Mom. Sorry to wake you. Michele's moving up the coast. It's a Category Three. Are you staying? Do you want to come here with ABS?"

...

"Okay. I'll call him right now and have him pick you guys up. Pack some food from your freezer. I have plenty of blankets. If you have extra water, have ABS get that too. Grab the blue tarps by the pool too. Okay, see you in a few hours. Be careful. Love you too."

Next I left a voice mail for ABS, "Hey. I know you're swamped. Is CaribSea closed? When you're finished can you run by and pick up my parents and Grams before you come up the beach? Thanks baby. Be safe! See you in a little bit. Love you."

ABS arrives a couple of hours later with my family. It took longer than usual as the wind has picked up and the rain is falling in torrents, making it almost impossible to see the ocean or the sound. Driving down the middle of the flooded road was the only way to get here.

"Roads are almost impassable and several streets have more than a foot of water running across them. The bridge supports will probably be ripped out. Let's double check all your windows and doors, Babe." I sense the urgency and concern in ABS' voice.

Journey grabs some towels and helps everyone dry off as ABS and I recheck the house.

"Journey and I got the Bahama shutters down, but I wish we'd put up plywood too," I say. "I should have put away the blankets the movers used when they delivered my deck furniture. They'll fly everywhere! They sure were in a hurry, and I don't blame them. It was nuts to deliver them last night with the storm coming right at us."

"Too late now baby, but we'll be fine."

"I'm sure, but this is really scaring me. I haven't been in a storm like this in years. And now…, living right on the beach… I wonder if we should we have evacuated?"

"Nothing to do now but sit tight. This time tomorrow it'll be over. You'll think it was just a dream. Promise!" Hugging me close he adds, "Let's go upstairs and join the party."

Grams and Journey, her only grandson, sip lemonade while Mom and Dad opt for more mature beverages. Everyone is glued to the television. A collective gasp escapes as the Storm Tracker Special Announcement interrupts the regularly scheduled news.

We interrupt our ongoing weather report to bring this emergency update. New models indicate Hurricane Michele has outer bands of sustained wind over one hundred and fifty-six miles per hour and is expected to make landfall on Bogue Banks. All people in the Channel 7 viewing area must seek shelter immediately. Landfall is anticipated between Atlantic Beach and the eastern edge of Bogue Banks, near Fort Macon, at seven o'clock tonight. Due to the expected high tide at eight o'clock, the storm surge may exceed fifteen feet. Prepare for flooding. Tornados and water spouts are possible, as is a power outage on the island. Do not venture outside for any reason. Injury or death from flying debris, drowning, or electrical shock are real possibilities. Local authorities warn: no emergency responders will come out until the storm passes. We repeat...

Journey's face is drained of color. My baby boy is shark-belly white. Grams huddles closer to Mom while Dad continues his limping pace, back and forth, across the dining area.

"Okay everyone, we just need to stay calm. Journey, honey it'll be alright. We have a sturdy house and plenty of supplies."

"But Mom, what about the sea turtles?" Journey cries. "Their nests are my responsibility. I bet no one covered them."

The lights flicker and fail. The increasing winds buffet the house while windows, doors, and ceilings creak and groan. Grams shrieks and Mom begins to cry silently, "We should have left. It's just like Hugo in '89."

"It's okay guys," Dad says peering out the window. "A transformer blew across the street. Our generator will be on in ten seconds. Ah. There it is now," as the lights come back on.

I'm so glad I put in the generator when we bought the house.

It's only five o'clock, but the early September sky is almost black. The rain continues to pour without letup, pelting the roof like machine gun fire. The television blares as Dad switches channels trying to get the most up to date information. I'm not sure it really matters what channel we watch tonight – they all say the same thing. Stay inside! Protect yourself and valuables. Stay safe and ride it out, if still on the island. What they aren't saying is how stupid we are to be here still.

In the back of my mind something clicks, and I ask quietly, at first, "Journey?" Then a little bit louder, "ABS, where's Journey?" Instinctively, I know. I race to the door screaming, "Journey, Journey, Journey."

Certainly he would not have gone out in this weather! But, ever since the lights went out, I have neither seen nor heard him. I yell for him through the rain and howling wind.

ABS and I are barely able to stand as we race around outside the house. We're instantly soaked as the wind-driven rain pushes us back against the house pilings. I can't find him. Journey's gone. Then I see it. Rather, I see where it should be. His scooter. Gone. The lock hangs loosely on the pole. "Nooooo. Journey. Noooo."

I know where he's headed.

"Mom, Dad, he's gone. Journey took his scooter and the tarps. He's going to Fort Macon to cover the turtle nests. He won't make it. He can't..."

ABS takes control and directs Dad. "Call 911. I'm going after him. I know where the nests are, near the edge of the fort. Call the Coast Guard station and ask them to look for him. And tell the Master Chief, Seal needs a boat."

It only takes Journey ten minutes to ride to the fort from our new house. In this weather, with the wind at his back, and no one else on the road, he might even make better time - if he doesn't get killed. No telling how long he was gone before I noticed, but he definitely has a head start. He could be there soon. Out in the open with the wind and rain....

"Oh, My God, help him," I pray.

ABS jumps into his truck. I dive into the passenger seat, before he can object.

"Go, go, go," I beg.

ABS races out of my driveway, fishtailing into the center of the road, now flooded with more than a foot of fast moving water. The hurricane force winds quickly push us up the coast reminding me that Journey is out here, unprotected, too. Surely ABS will catch Journey riding out here alone on his scooter.

The rain bites and stings my face as I lean out to check the side of the road. I don't really want to find Journey there and I wonder how he could have made it this far with the road flooded and the wind so strong.

ABS hydroplanes across the road and barrels into the Coast Guard station where Master Chief Boyce anxiously waits at the dock, wearing his foul weather gear.

Dad got through to him, obviously.

Through the wind I hear him yell, "Seal, you're crazy. It's a suicide mission. But it's your suicide. I'll see you on the beach."

ABS jumps on the high powered Coast Guard rescue jet ski and heads into the choppy water. The Master Chief signals me to get into his military tracked vehicle. In a few minutes we find the Fort Macon gate, locked. There is still a faint scooter track indicating Journey drove around the gate.

"Damn," the chief exclaims as he holds me back in my seat with his outstretched right arm. He rams the gate. Nothing happens. He rolls back and attacks again. This time the gate bends and pulls free from the loose sand. He drives right over it. Wind-aided, in a few minutes we drive onto the beach. Even with tracks, it is too difficult to drive further. We see Journey's scooter laid down, not far from where we entered.

ABS made great time, too, considering the elements. I see him coming around the point, fighting to progress in the churning water. No one else would be out here. Fifteen foot waves pummel him, but he promised as we drove that he, "Wasn't going to let Journey die."

Chief and I see the jet ski spotlight bobbing through the waves. In the blinding wind and sand we also see Journey futilely working to cover his nests. He's trying to protect them with the blue tarps and wooden stakes. I see the first two nests he covered. The wind has ripped those stakes out of the sand and shredded the tarp. Journey must be oblivious as he kneels and works on the third one.

We struggle to reach him against the whipping wind and soaked sand. A trench of racing surf cuts inward, stretches the width of the beach, and blocks our effort. There is no way to wade through it. It would take too long to go back and around. We yell to Journey, but he doesn't respond. All we can do is watch this drama unfold and hope ABS reaches him in time.

Covered by sand, certainly cold, and feeling the sand sting his body, Journey appears disoriented. He knows right where it's supposed to be. But the "here" is now under three feet of swirling cold, dark water. Where minutes ago was sand, the waves crash against his waist. Journey appears frozen in place.

ABS plan is to ground the jet ski on the beach, grab Journey, and run back to the station using the fort road. Huge, hungry waves race at him from all directions trying to rip him from his craft. Shining his search light, apparently ABS sees Journey crouching near the water's edge. ABS pushes through the waves toward his objective.

Chief and I see what unfolds, but are powerless to help. Journey stands up as we continue to scream, "Journey, Journey, Journey." He glances in our direction. It seems like he may hear us. But, the rising water is now up to his chest. Journey struggles to stay upright.

"Help. I'm here. Help," he calls out, his teenage voice nearly drowned by the winds and water. Journey finds himself being sucked out to sea, as if in a riptide. He's in trouble, being tossed upside down and around like a towel in a washing machine. "Hlp. Hp.. h...," Journey struggles to yell through the murky and brackish water, soon to be his grave. Gasping for a breath, he fearfully waves in our direction. It appears he sees us on the beach, but we're now nearly a quarter mile away. Between us is an ocean of water. He disappears.

ABS must have seen the same thing as he makes a bee-line toward the spot. Moments later, Journey reappears, bouncing across the tops of the waves, being pulled toward deep, open water. Turning back into the angry chop, ABS pushes his jet ski and himself. He races toward the young man he hopes will one day be his son. He guns the throttle and races toward what looks like a body being tossed about like a rag doll. Closing on the object, he realizes it's not Journey. Suddenly, a mammoth wave rocks ABS from behind, lifting him over the water, and propelling him into the channel marker buoy.

As soon as the winds die enough, Dad drives to the Coast Guard station to be with Kirby. Master Chief Boyce, who stayed with Kirby on the beach, consoles her as best as he can. "I'm so sorry Ma'am. There's no sign of either of them or the jet ski. We'll launch helicopters at dawn and continue searching."

Exhausted, I sit before I fall. Within seconds I'm out. As I regain consciousness, I hear, faintly at first, then growing louder, "…mom, Mom MOM, **MOM, wake up!**

Chapter 23

Alive

"... **M**OM wake up. Are you okay? I have your pretzel and drink. You were really out of it. I think they're calling our names for our flight."

"Journey. You're alive!"

"Mom, what are you talking about? You look like you saw a ghost. Are you okay?"

"Oh Journey," interrupting him. I stumble out of the rocking chair and hug him harder than ever. Rubbing his back and patting his hair, I offer a quiet prayer, "Thank You, God." I say to Journey, "I'm so sorry for scaring you. I must have fallen asleep. My dream... It was so real!"

"Are you sure Mom? Do you need EMS?"

"No, I'm fine. It's just...never mind. Seriously, I'm really fine." Seeing the pretzels in his hand I add, "Let's roll. I can eat on the plane."

Racing through the terminal, I spy a special needs passenger cart. Unlady-like, I flag down the driver. He stops, perhaps because of my disheveled appearance, or maybe he just doesn't want to hit me. Hurriedly, I explain our

predicament. The white-haired, elderly, southern gentle-
men replies, "Hop on missus, son."

The Charlotte NASCAR family has nothing on this
driver as he speeds through the terminal, honking his horn
endlessly, sending travelers and airport workers scurrying
for safety. Over the noise and commotion, I hear him say
into his shoulder mounted walkie-talkie something about
"VIPs inbound" and to "hold the plane."

As fast as it began, our dash through the airport
screeches to a halt. Our driver jumps out and muscles our
bags off the cart. Hurrying ahead, he yells to the uniformed agent beginning to close the jet way door, "Hold
the door. Hold the door. VIPs boarding."

Ignoring him, she continues pulling it closed. Less
than a few feet separate us from our last flight home as I
rush the door. Finally, it slowly swings the opposite way
as an exasperated flight attendant quickly ushers us onto
the plane.

"Take any seat. Just sit down – we're ready to take off."

We practically run down the aisle and take the remaining two seats. This time they are in the very back of
the cramped commuter plane. I don't care. I want to kiss
the seat – we were so close to missing the flight. Waiting
for us longer than they should have, the pilot completes a
quick taxi and accelerates down the runway. My seatbelt is
not fastened and my carry-on is on my lap. I gasp loudly
as the abrupt takeoff forces me back in my seat. I look
around at other passengers, who seemed agitated when we

boarded, and notice a shaggy, brown-haired young man sitting across the aisle in front of us.

Angling a tanned face slightly to the left, he looks at us and smiles. "Y'all okay?" he asks with a charming southern drawl mixed with a touch of Cajun that would melt butter.

"Yes. We're fine now," I reply. "Thank you."

My heart skips a beat as his smile broadens from cheek to cheek. "That's good... Real good, ma'am."

So polite. He sounds strangely familiar. I just can't place it.

Extending his hand across the aisle, he tips the brim of his well-loved, straw cowboy hat, and adds, "My name's Andrew Bradham. People just call me... Andy. Pleased to meet you."

Author Biography

Thomas P. Gill is a retired Air Force officer and health-care executive.

Gill was raised in Statesville, North Carolina. He graduated from East Carolina University and entered the US Air Force. During his Air Force career, Gill worked with nuclear missiles, taught at the Military College of South Carolina, and managed a military accessions organization. He also received his master's degree in operations management.

Gill now lives in Emerald Isle, North Carolina. He enjoys working with writers' groups, playing golf, going to the beach, and volunteering with turtle-patrol programs and local foundations.

Gill married his high-school sweetheart. They enjoy spending time with their two daughters, son-in-law, and granddaughter. Gill's first book, *The Bridge*, was based on a true story. He is now revisiting the lives of his characters with its sequel, *Return to Emerald Isle*.